The Wisterious Witch

A Cozy Mystery (Wisterious Bay Cozy Paranormal Mystery Book 1)

Ileana Muñoz Renfroe

Published by Ileana Muñoz Renfroe, 2022.

Copyright

Copyright © 2022 Ileana Muñoz Renfroe

All rights reserved.

ISBN Ebook: 979-8-9867450-0-8

ISBN Paperback: 979-8-9867450-6-0

Library of Congress: 2022916793

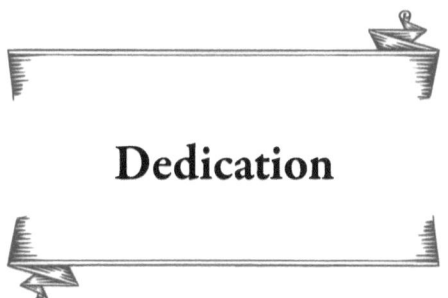

Dedication

To my children, the love of my life, who despite all my quirks still love me. You are the reason I wake up every morning. And for Eleanor for bringing me love, joy, and laughter every day.

Acknowledgments

To my family who support me even when they don't think they do and accept that I'm a bit different and sort of kooky.

To all of my beta readers, words cannot express my gratitude.

A special thanks to Heather Doyle Harrisson, P.A. you rock. To Jennifer and Patricia, and especially Elena Bluntzer for her hospitality. The perfect place for summer writing and hanging out with old and new friends.

To my Facebook Community Group, Cozy Mystery Village, and my Reading Group, for being so supportive during my journey. You are all truly remarkable, thank you.

To the readers who make this all possible, and all the librarians and booksellers who ignite people's passion for reading.

To my mother and father who I know are smiling down on me from heaven.

And last, but certainly not least, thank you always to my grandmother Rosa, my Nana and my inspiration.

CAST OF CHARACTERS

Alicia Whimblebright - Witch
 Felix – Humorous talking skeleton
Augustus – Banished reaper
Zoraida – Alicia's kitten
Meredith – Cousin/prima and owner of Hannah's Tea House
Hannah – Meredith's deceased mother and previous owner of Hannah's Tea House
Gertrude – Employee at Patchouli Mystical Tesoros Shop
Valentino – Gertrude's cousin
Catalina – Owner of Catalina's Hair Salon
Haydee – Alicia's neighbor
Laura – Coven leader
Sheriff McDonald
Deputy Donaldson
Ralph Henderson - Coroner
Heather – Owner of The Maple Crumb Cake Bakery
Sebastian Sunbean - Solicitor
Sam – Town flirt
Dolores – Sam's girlfriend

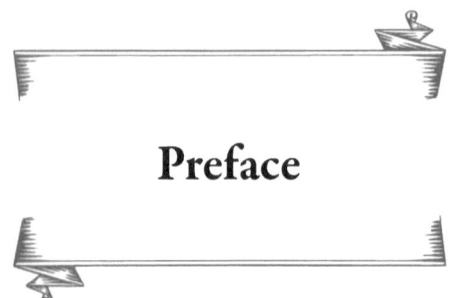

Preface

After many years of dreaming about writing a cozy mystery I finally took the plunge and started to put all the pieces together. The story of Rosa the Cuban Psychic was inspired partly by my Grandmother Rosa and the fact that I was raised in a Cuban household.

The stories come to me from reading an article online, having someone tell me a story, or sometimes just people watching. The characters are fun to create and develop. I hope you'll follow me on my journey and enjoy my books.

If you've liked what I have written, then please take a few minutes to leave a review on Amazon and don't forget to visit my website for updates. Stay tuned for my next book coming soon.

Happy reading.

I.M. Renfroe

https://www.imrenfroe.com

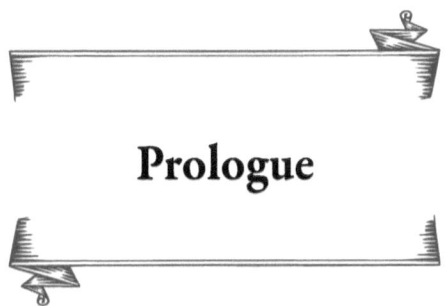

Prologue

Alicia found herself lost. She hated her job and her life and knew she needed a complete change. What she didn't realize was that her wish was about to come true. Wisterious Bay was enchanting and magical. Now, even with the dead bodies, Alicia couldn't imagine living anywhere else in this world.

Chapter 1

Traditions abound in Wisterious Bay, and this year was no exception. As the curator and owner of Patchouli Mystical Tesoros, Alicia, a precarious witch, was in charge of creating and displaying sought after crystals, artifacts from around the world, and most importantly her one-of-a-kind enchanted candles.

She was in her mid-thirties, from Cuban descent, excited about her new ideas for the coming year and overall satisfied with her life. One thing was certain, she hadn't been looking for change.

If Alicia had thought about the exact time and place where her life had altered irrevocably, you would think it would've been the day a solicitor appeared at her doorstep. But no, that wasn't the day. Instead, it was precisely at seven-thirty on the third of October.

Actually, the solicitor showing up unexpectedly was quite a shock. It all started on one rainy day a few years back. She was at home, in the kitchen, making her *special* candles when there was a knock on her door. Walking over to see who could be disturbing her so early in the morning, she peeked through the eye slot to see a man in a brown uniform wearing a cap, and holding what appeared to be a long yellow envelope.

Feeling he had knocked on the wrong apartment, she slightly opened the door and was about to tell him that when he asked her name.

"Are you Ms. Alicia Whimblebright?"

"Si, yo me llamo Alicia Whimblebright. Sorry, yes, that's me," she replied, eying the envelope in his hand.

"Special delivery. Please sign here," he said as he handed her a tablet to sign.

As she signed the tablet and before she could ask who the envelope was from, he tapped his cap.

"Thank you and have a nice day," he turned around and walked away.

Closing the door Alicia wondered who could be sending her something let alone mandándole a ella un sobre? Who would've been sending her an envelope that required a special delivery? It's not as if she'd known anyone important.

Going back into the kitchen she sat at the table and turned the envelope over a few times. *It looks like it's from some kind of firm as it has three names, interesante,* she thought to herself.

Shrugging, she proceeded to open the envelope along the flap. She extracted a letter that looked rather fancy, placing it on the table to read.

Ms. Alicia Whimblebright,

We are very sorry to have to inform you of your father's death. As solicitors to your father's estate, we want to express our condolences to you on his passing.

There will be a reading of the will in two days at precisely ten-o-clock in the morning. I cannot urge you enough how important it is that you attend.

Looking forward to meeting you in person.

Until then, yours truly,

Sebastian Sunbean,

Solicitor to the Whimblebright estate

Alicia considered not attending as she couldn't imagine what her father could've left her, especially since she didn't even remember him. He had never been part of her life. As a matter of fact, all her mother had ever said about him was: *tu Papi was a good man, a good father, and he will be missed.*

Curiosity got the better of her, and she decided she needed to at least find out what they had to say. Not expecting much, she arrived early that day for the reading of the will.

After giving her name to the receptionist, she was asked to step into the conference room and await her solicitor. A few minutes later a rather short and stocky man walked in and introduced himself as Mr. Sunbean.

"But you can call me Sebastian if you wish," he stated.

Sebastian sat across the table and opened a file folder. Inside that folder was a large envelope that he slowly removed revealing several documents.

He then looked up at Alicia and started the proceedings. Having stated the date and time, Sebastian read the will out loud. He then detailed every item, of every document, and what each one entailed. Everything was happening too quickly. For Alicia it was somewhat overwhelming as never in her dreams did, she expect anything, let alone the number of items listed.

After the will was read, she learned she was the only heir from the Whimblebright clan. This meant she had inherited all of her Papi's assets. They included a home, several buildings on Main Street, a stipend that had grown into the millions, oh, and a large number of acres all in Wisterious Bay, a town she hadn't even ever heard of before meeting Mr. Sunbean.

Alicia had suddenly become a very wealthy woman.

She asked Sebastian if he could continue to monitor the estate, as she had no clue how to proceed. He agreed and she then signed all the necessary documents. As she walked out the door, she thanked him again for everything and told him she'd be reaching out soon with questions. For now, she just wanted to soak in the moment.

A few days later she logged into her checking account online, and sure enough, there were a lot of zeros. More than she could've possibly imagined she'd have at her disposal.

So, with no love interest, a car that was falling apart, and a job she hated, Alicia went shopping. The first thing she did with her inheritance was purchase a new car. Nothing fancy, just something relatively inexpensive she could drive to Wisterious Bay without any problems. Then she purchased some new outfits. She couldn't show up in her old raggedy clothes. Satisfied with her purchases, and once everything was settled, she turned in her apartment rental keys and headed out to her new life.

When she first moved to Wisterious Bay, she didn't know anyone, but everyone was so welcoming that she soon felt right at home. Alicia learned that her Papi spoke of her often to the townspeople. He even followed her on her social media page.

Obviously, none of this Alicia knew beforehand. She thought he had abandoned them when she was a little girl. It turns out that was not the case. He left because if he had stayed, he believed his family would've been in danger. So, her parents decided the only way to protect Alicia was for him to leave before anyone knew he had a family. To this day, Alicia still does not know what danger they thought they were protecting her from or why they did what they did. All she did know was that she missed out on getting to know her Papi.

Someday, she vowed to find out the truth. For now, she'd take one day at a time.

Now that her Mami and Papi had passed away, it was time to take her rightful place in the Whimblebright family line. It did feel strange learning about her Papi from strangers and not from her Mami. But the more she learned, the more she realized her Papi had been a great man.

Mami taught her everything about her culture. Being raised in a Cuban house full of witches had its ups and downs, but mostly ups. Imagine a house with three Cuban witches all with very different personalities.

Alicia laughed whenever she thought about her family, especially all in one room discussing a new spell. She missed those days. Her Mami and tias had all passed away leaving her completely alone.

As far as she knew there were no relatives remaining from her mother's side. Alicia promised her Mami at her deathbed to continue the tradition, and if she ever did have any children, she'd teach them the same way she was taught.

So, with a new life ahead of her, she established herself in Wisterious Bay. She made sure she introduced herself as the landlord to the many buildings she now owned. As it so happens, shortly after arriving in Wisterious Bay, one of the tenants passed away, and Alicia took this opportunity to open up her Patchouli Mystical Tesoros Shop, something she had always dreamt of doing someday.

Now, three years later, she had friends, she was part of a coven, and she was overall liked by everyone in Wisterious Bay, or at least that's what she'd thought.

Every morning, she hightailed herself to The Cauldron Coffee Shop to meet two of her coven sisters for coffee and gossip. It was the only time she could spare before the start of her day.

This morning she showered early and donned a long sleeve shirt, jeans, and walking shoes. As she left her house, she grabbed her jacket and noticed the weather had started to become chilly. The leaves were changing. The foliage was at its peak. This was her favorite time of the year, October.

Smiling she turned the collar up and pulled her jacket closer to her body as she headed into town. The walk was not too long, as her house was just about a mile from Main Street.

During this time of year, the streets were adorned with orange lanterns, garlands, twinkling orange lights, skeletons hanging from light posts, and more pumpkins than she could count, all placed in various locations throughout town. Everyone in Wisterious Bay got into the craze of Halloween.

Usually, during the early hours she'd wave Hola and Buenos Dias to the joggers she'd see running. As she approached Main Street, she'd also see the shop owners getting ready to open up their shops. They'd all smile and wave back in return. Alicia especially enjoyed the aroma coming from the bakery as her mouth undoubtedly watered every time.

One of the perks about the month of October, was the market. Alicia believed strongly in promoting the local businesses, so she'd always buy several items from the local vendors. Many of them took this opportunity to sell their spicy pumpkin bread, pumpkin spice latte, and well, you get the drift, all things pumpkin.

This particular morning, Alicia reminded herself she needed to pick up some of the pumpkin bread for the shop before heading to The Cauldron Coffee Shop. Besides serving the pumpkin spice coffee for free during the month, she also provided samplings of the bread for her customers. It was another way to help promote the local bakery shop.

When she thought of The Patchouli Mystical Tesoros Shop, it made her happy. This was her haven. Inside, the walls on three sides had been painted a light color of sage offsetting the duck egg blue behind the counter. It was her happy place.

There was a dedicated section to the right of the cash register where she placed the pumpkin bread and the coffee machine. Local customers knew to come in and serve themselves. A treat she enjoyed providing.

Alicia had spent all year preparing her shop for Halloween. The month-long celebration started at the beginning of October and concluded with the final event on the last day of the month. There were tours of haunted homes, fun activities, and the immersion of the tourists that descended to the quaint town all wanting to participate in the festivities.

Wisterious Bay, a hidden gem, was a small town nestled in the heart of Boston's North Shore inhabited by humans and witches alike. Although most humans living there didn't know about the witches. They kept their coven a secret and their outdoor rituals hidden from plain view.

As she entered the Maple Crumb Cake Bakery, she was overpowered by the aroma. Her stomach growled as she approached the counter.

"Good morning, Alicia," the girl behind the counter said with a smile.

"Buenos Dias. Tell me about the specials because if this aroma is any indication of what you guys have created today, I'm taking the whole lot," she giggled as she rubbed her hands together.

"Well, I must admit it's a heavenly combination. Today's special is one Heather has created especially for this time of year. She's calling it Mystical Delight. It's a mouth-watering mini crumb cake that's perfect with a pumpkin latte or a pumpkin spice tea. Would you like a sample?" she asked, already grabbing a piece knowing Alicia couldn't resist.

"As if you have to ask," Alicia replied while making a goofy face.

The moment Alicia tasted the mini crumb cake she made moaning sounds that had the patrons sitting at the nearby table giggling.

"Oh my, this is amazing. Que delicioso! It melts in my mouth. I must have a dozen for the shop and one for me ahora mismo!" she chuckled.

Smiling, the girl behind the counter turned and started gathering the pastries.

Alicia checked her watch and confirmed she still had plenty of time to drop off the mini crumb cakes at her shop, so she sat at one of the empty tables and took her time eating her mini crumb cake while she waited for her order.

She said hello to several of the local townspeople sitting at the nearby tables. They chatted a bit about the upcoming festivities. Those that had shops had already started to advertise around town. Their windows were decorated with Halloween garlands and candles on the windowsill.

The others who didn't own a business in town, participated in the marketplace events by either showcasing their handmade creations, cooking or baking, or even helping around town.

Wisterious Bay was definitely the only place on Earth where Alicia knew everyone participated in all of the local events. Of course, you always had those who gossiped and loved the drama or were just plain mean. She tried her best to stay away from those individuals as they only brought trouble.

The front door suddenly jingled indicating someone had entered. Alicia looked up to see a man in his mid-thirties dressed in a bespoke black suit. He had broad shoulders, onyx black hair, and piercing blue eyes. For a moment her heart stopped.

When his eyes met hers, Alicia knew she was in trouble.

He nodded and proceeded to the counter. She hung onto his every word.

"Good morning, welcome to The Maple Crumb Cake Bakery. What can I get for you today?" the girl behind the counter said as she smiled.

"I would like to buy a box of your baked goods. Maybe a sampling of your best?" he said with a sultry voice. At least that's how it sounded to Alicia.

"Of course. I'll put together some of our best, including this month's special. It's our mini crumb cake. Everyone seems to love it."

"Perfect, thank you," he answered, looking around the bakery as he spoke.

"By the way, I've never seen you here. Are you just passing by?"

Laughing he looked around again focusing on Alicia for a split second before responding. Turning around, he smiled.

"Yes and no. I'm here to visit someone," he replied rather vaguely.

"Oh, well hope she enjoys these."

"What makes you think it's a woman?" he smiled with a twinkle in his eyes.

"Because men don't usually go into a bakery and buy sweets for a man. Well, wait, that's not true," she answered rather aghast.

"No worries. Yes, it's for a female," he replied laughing as he was enjoying the back-and-forth dialogue.

"Boy, for a moment I thought I had insulted you. Sorry about that. I really should mind my own business. Let me just finish your order," she said as she hurried away.

"Take your time," he replied smiling. He then turned around again.

Alicia tried to act as if she wasn't staring at him, but she made such a ruckus by almost choking on her mini crumb cake, he laughed.

"Are you alright there?" he asked.

"Yes, sorry. I, a, I," Alicia stumbled and blushed, giving up on trying to explain anything. *Por Dios*, she thought to herself. *Can I act any more foolish?*

"As long as you're alright," he answered, smiling, trying to make her more uncomfortable than she was already.

He felt it too, a pull of some kind. The attraction and electricity between them was there without question. It was evident when he placed his hand on her shoulder to steady her.

Alicia was so shocked by the zap she actually stumbled back and fell right on her tush.

Everyone in the coffee shop watched the whole event unfold before their eyes. No one dared move as it was obvious something had just happened between them. The sparks were there for everyone to see. They tried, however, to act as if nothing special had happened.

Alicia stood up and brushed herself off claiming the chair was unsteady. He just nodded and was about to say something when the girl at the counter called his name letting him know his order was ready.

At the same time Alicia's name was called and she, too, walked up to the counter. They stood alongside each other avoiding physical contact, each afraid they would be zapped again.

Alicia extended her hand indicating he should go first. Thanking her, he paid for his box. He then turned around and wished Alicia a good day before heading out the door.

"Boy, what happened?" asked the girl behind the counter.

"What do you mean, what happened?" Alicia asked, still shaken.

"The spark. The tension. The heat!" the girl behind the counter replied.

"Oh please. You've been watching too much television. There was nothing there and I'm sure we'll never see him again after this morning," Alicia replied, hoping against all odds that he was not just passing by or coming into town to meet a girlfriend.

Stop Alicia, she told herself. What was she thinking? She needed to get a grip. Taking a deep breath, she smiled and paid for her order. Alicia walked out wishing everyone a great day just as *Love is In The Air* began to play over the speaker.

Oh yeah, she was in trouble.

Alicia Whimblebright caught a glimpse of herself in the window. She was thirty-four and in fairly good health. Tall, with bright red hair and green eyes, she had a special twinkle in her eye when she looked at you, almost as if she could read into your soul. The red hair came from her father's side. The tan skin and green eyes from her mother. A Cuban and an Irishman, a winning combination. Still single, she had given up on love a long time ago.

Every once in a while, she wished there was a significant other in her life. But just as quickly she disregarded the thought. She figured if she was meant to have someone in her life it would've already happened. Instead, she settled for a familiar.

Every witch she knew had a cat. But not Alicia, no, she ended up with a reaper and a skeleton that came to life after dark. Go figure.

Chapter 2

The Maple Crumb Cake Bakery started off making crumb cakes when they first opened their doors. But eventually, as it happens with everything in life, they started experimenting and expanding.

The next thing they knew, everyone was asking for more and more of their baked goods. Delighted they continued to create different pastries, cakes, scones, and desserts.

By then, they had established a brand and since everyone knew them as the crumb cake bakery, they decided why change what was working. So, Heather kept the name and only changed the offerings.

As Alicia walked out of The Maple Crumb Cake Bakery, she noticed down the street in front of the local newspaper two people clearly speaking loudly.

"That is not what we had agreed upon."

"Yes, it is. We both decided that it would be best if."

"Stop right there. I'm not stupid. I know what this is all about and I'm not accepting whatever you were about to say."

As Alicia looked closer, she realized it was Laura, the president of her coven. The other person she couldn't really see because they had their back to her and were bundled up in a jacket she didn't recognize.

Not wanting to appear as if she had eavesdropped, Alicia pulled up her collar and decided to look away and act as if she hadn't noticed anything unusual. She had slowly begun to walk towards her shop when she turned around and glanced at the two arguing. That's when she noticed Laura frowning. Her beautiful green eyes suddenly snapped and she looked like a serpent staring down at her prey. Startled she was about to interfere, but decided against it. Whatever was going on she didn't want to get involved.

Alicia quickly increased her steps and headed away from them hoping they hadn't noticed her. Indeed, neither one had noticed her.

Her shop was just two doors down so she arrived quickly. She was still thinking about the delicious mini crumb cake when she approached her front door.

Distracted she hadn't noticed someone was in her shop talking to Gertrude, her employee. Gertrude usually liked to be in the shop early to rearrange shelves, fix up the display window if needed, and get the shop ready to open.

As Alicia inserted her key, knowing it would be locked this early in the morning, she noticed both Gertrude and the other person turn around.

Her heart stopped yet again. Twice in the same day.

The man that had been at The Maple Crumb Cake Bakery was standing in her shop. Talking nonetheless to Gertrude. Holding the box of pastries, he had just purchased.

As she slowly opened the door, instead of looking at them, she looked up to see the jingling bells she had placed on the frame of the door to let her know when someone entered. She dared not make eye contact with the man. She was afraid; she'd do something foolish.

"Alicia. I'm so glad you stopped by this morning before your coffee get-together," Gertrude said smiling.

"Yes. I stopped by the bakery and was just dropping off the pastries before meeting the girls. Don't let me interrupt you," she replied while looking directly at the man.

Smiling he started to extend his hand and pulled it back immediately. Gertrude didn't notice the exchange, but Alicia did.

"Hello. Let me formally introduce myself. I'm Valentino," he said as he smiled.

"Alicia, this is my cousin from my father's side," Gertrude said pointing at Valentino.

"I'm not certain if you realize my father is from Spain and my mother is from right here in Wisterious Bay. They met one year when she studied abroad, fell in love and as the saying goes, the rest is history," she continued smiling at both Valentino and Alicia.

"Very nice to meet you, Valentino," Alicia replied as she felt butterflies dancing in her stomach.

She knew there were no such things as real butterflies in your stomach. However, she could've sworn they were real at that moment.

"We actually sort of met already at the bakery. I stopped to pick up these pastries for you when she fell off her chair and I helped her up," he said, looking at Gertrude and avoiding Alicia's gaze.

Now that's not how she remembered the incident. But if he needed to fib, who was she to argue with him. Aww, who's she kidding?

"That's not exactly how it happened. Yes, he walked into the bakery. However, I did not just fall, the chair was faulty. He gallantly helped me up and that was that," she tried not to appear as if she had just told a lie.

Now she felt foolish. It was obvious she couldn't be around him. She needed to know if she had to run away now.

"So, how long are you staying in town?" Alicia wondered.

"That's just what I was asking him. We haven't seen each other in several years and I'm hoping he can stay for a while," Gertrude answered before Valentino could respond.

"Well, I'm actually staying indefinitely," he replied without thinking.

Now why would he say that? He thought to himself.

"That's great news!" Gertrude replied clapping her hands.

Hay Dios Mio, Alicia thought to herself.

Guess he needed to find a realtor and look into some property. He could stay for a few months and see what all the fuss is about in Wisterious Bay. He couldn't help but notice the moment he arrived in town, all the signs related to the Halloween celebrations. There were a few other things in town he was interested in checking out. All of these things were going through his mind as he continued to stare at

Alicia. Something about her was enchanting, mysterious, and possibly dangerous.

"Yes, great news," Alicia repeated as she looked down at her feet. Now she was worried. This man was definitely a distraction she hadn't expected. All she had to do was stay out of his way. That was something she could do. She'd been alone for so long it would be easy. Besides she had no time for romance.

"Alicia, come see what I did with the display," Gertrude encouraged Alicia to see what she had done, as she walked around the main counter.

"What do you think?" asked Gertrude as she stood by the cash register.

The pleasing aroma of the combination of scented candles that filled the room and the beautiful display created by Gertrude made her forget about Valentino for a split moment.

She leaned in, breathed in deep, and looked up before responding.

"Wow, I never would've thought about lighting both of these candles together. I think we have a new scent in the works," Alicia smiled.

"Right? I wanted to play around and see how it'd do before we opened today and after a few minutes of the candles being lit, I realized this was an amazing scent you needed to make happen," Gertrude replied smiling.

"And your display is on point. Great job as always. Let's work on this new scent over the weekend if you're free?" Alicia asked.

"Thank you. Absolutely. You know you can always count on me," Gertrude smiled in return.

"Since your cousin has just arrived in town, why don't you take the day off and spend it with him," she encouraged Gertrude mostly because she didn't want him popping in to distract her. She had too much work to do and didn't need the interruption.

"We have so much that still has to be done," Gertrude argued. She didn't want Alicia feeling as if she had abandoned her.

"Don't be silly. I can handle it. I'm going now for coffee and I'll be back in plenty of time to open the shop. You go have fun and catch up," she said to Gertrude continuing to avoid looking at Valentino.

"Alright, then if, you are sure. I will stop by later just in case," Gertrude replied as she grabbed her coat.

"NO!" Alicia said rather loudly startling Gertrude. Valentino grinned.

"Aw, alright? I won't stop by?" Gertrude Shrugged not certain why Alicia was behaving that way. Realizing Alicia was not going to change her mind she nodded in agreement.

"Well then, thanks again and see you tomorrow," she hugged Alicia and grabbed Valentino as they headed out the door.

"See you tomorrow," Alicia called out as the door closed.

Yup! She was definitely in trouble.

Taking a deep breath, she walked to the back kitchen and placed the box of pastries in the fridge. Later, she would take them out and warm them before placing them on the counter for the customers.

For now, she blew out the candles, made a note of creating the new scent, locked the door and headed out to meet her coven sisters for a much-needed coffee and gossip session at The Cauldron Coffee Shop before she needed to return to open her shop.

All the stores she frequented were on Main Street and within walking distance. So, she didn't have to travel very far to get to her destination. Walking less than a mile radius she arrived at the coffee shop.

Taking a deep breath, she opened the door to the coffee shop and walked in. Sitting in the corner were a few of the coven sisters. They didn't really like getting up so early in the morning, and that was obvious by the carafe of coffee and rubbing of eyes. Two tables down were her two regulars; Laura and Meredith.

As she walked toward her table, she was told their orders would be right up. She smiled, thanked her, and then said hi to everyone in the coffee shop and she approached her table and sat down. Laura, sat there as if nothing had happened even though Alicia had seen her arguing with someone earlier.

"Good morning, Laura. Good morning, Meredith," Alicia said to both of them.

"Good morning," they replied in unison.

Alicia had joined the Salem Coven by chance. The first time she heard the name she thought how original, not. But her cousin Meredith, also a witch had lived in Wisterious Bay all her life and encouraged her to attend a meeting after she moved into town.

It never crossed her mind to join a coven. Most of the time she practiced her craft on her own having learned what she did from her mother. Since she created magical candles that was something she didn't share with anyone. Eventually they changed her mind and convinced her being part of a coven was the right thing to do.

Basically, they explained it to Alicia so that she'd clearly understand When you joined the coven you entered a very special group where each one swore to protect each member as you would protect yourself. By being part of that exclusive group, also gave you some of their strength, and together as you can imagine they were very powerful. It also gave one the opportunity to perfect their craft.

So, when Meredith told her the benefits of the coven and what a great bunch of people were in it, she decided why not.

At first when she joined it was only females, but the last few years they'd opened up the coven to warlocks also and that has made it much more interesting. Not surprisingly, it's been a great union. In fact, Laura had recently informed the coven how she was thinking of stepping down from that role because she wanted to travel. By having someone else step in as president, it allowed her the freedom she craved.

The morning get-together for coffee though remained a girl thing. No men allowed.

"So, what news do we have to share?" Meredith asked.

No one answered.

"Hello, are you guys here?" she looked from Laura to Alicia arching her eyebrows.

"Sorry, no news this morning," Laura answered appearing distracted.

Alicia thought about the heated argument she heard earlier and wondered if that was what was causing Laura to appear distant.

"And you?" Meredith asked looking at Alicia.

"Me? Well, let's see. I'm giving Gertrude the day off, but that's about it," she answered avoiding making eye contact.

Meredith looked at Alicia with narrowed eyes.

"I know you enough to know there's more to this story. So, spill it now," Meredith demanded as she placed her crossed hands on the table.

Laura remained silent.

"Gertrude's cousin is in town and I thought it would be nice if they spend the day catching up. She hasn't seen him in several years," she replied trying to force a smile.

"That's interesting. I don't know if that's all there is to it, but sooner or later I'll prod it out of you. So, be warned. Now, is he good looking? What does he do for a living? How long is he staying? Me estas oyendo?" Meredith looked directly at Alicia who at this point was looking down at her hands.

Meredith had decided the moment she met Alicia that she wanted to learn Spanish. That gave them an edge in town because not everyone spoke the language and this allowed them sometimes to discuss things in public without anyone knowing what they were saying.

Arching her eyebrows Alicia laughed.

"Wow, how much coffee have you had this morning, and yes I'm listening," Alicia chuckled.

"Too much, I guess. But don't avoid the questions, spill," Meredith crossed her arms and waited.

"Not sure what he does for a living. Apparently, he's staying for a short time, but I don't know how long. And, I guess yes, you could say he's rather cute, didn't really notice," she lied and again tried to avoid making eye contact with Meredith. She knew if she did it was over. She'd know immediately she was hiding something.

"Well, we'll have to see about that. I'm sure we'll find out more about him soon enough," Meredith said trying not to sound agitated. She let it go for now.

"As for me, if any of you are interested, I am working on a new tea line for the shop. As owner of Hannah's Tea House, I have a reputation to uphold and cannot let my poor deceased mother down. She'd be turning in her grave if I didn't do a stellar job with the shop," Meredith sighed.

"You'll be fine. Hannah would not be turning in her grave. In fact, she'd be very proud of you for everything you've done with the shop. Everything you do there comes out wonderfully. Don't forget to let me know when you have something new so that I can add it to my inventory at the shop," Alicia smiled as she took a sip from her coffee.

"Thank you. That's why I love you guys. You always make me feel good even when I doubt myself. You always pick me up," Meredith grabbed Laura and Alicia's hands and squeezed. She then took a bite from her slice of toast and sipped her coffee.

That seemed to do the trick.

"I'm sorry. What did I miss?" Laura asked focusing her attention back to both of them.

Alicia and Meredith looked at each other and slightly shrugged.

"Meredith was telling us about a new tea shipment and how excited she was about trying out some new combinations. She was thanking us for always having her back," Alicia said as she smiled.

"Oh, that's wonderful news Meredith. Congratulations! I'm sure whatever you put together will be a huge success," Laura replied.

"Are you alright Laura?" Alicia asked while taking a bit from her croissant.

"Yes, I just have a slight headache today. I'm sorry ladies, but I have to cut this morning's coffee get-together short. I'll see you both later," Laura said as she stood.

She placed some money on the table for her coffee and croissant which she never touched, and left without another word.

"What was that all about? I've never seen Laura behave that way. I hope everything is alright?" Meredith asked finishing up her coffee.

"I'm not certain. I did see her just before I came in here having a heated conversation with someone. I couldn't tell who it was as they had their back to me and I didn't recognize the coat the other person was wearing. I don't think she saw me as she didn't mention anything," Alicia replied.

"Who could she have been arguing with?" Meredith wondered.

"Not sure, but she looked upset. And no, I couldn't tell what they were arguing about," Alicia responded before Meredith could ask.

They remained silent for a few minutes each lost in their own thoughts.

"Well, I guess I don't have any other news to share. Today promises to be a very busy day. So, I'm going to head out. Esta bien?" Meredith asked.

"Si claro, let's go," Alicia responded as she drank what remained of her coffee and then stood.

Together they walked up to the counter to pay their bill.

"Was everything to your satisfaction?"

"Yes, of course. Thank you. We just have so much to do today. Laura had to run out and I have a delivery soon," Meredith replied not wanting them to think there was something wrong with her order.

Alicia had been standing behind her waiting to pay for her bill. When it was her turn, she was asked the same question.

"How was everything?"

"Excellent as usual. I have designed some new scents. You must stop by when you have a chance," Alicia said smiling.

"Wonderful to hear. That's sounds like a deal. I'll stop by later today."

"Perfect, see you then," Alicia replied and headed out with Meredith.

When they reached the outside, they hugged and kissed each other. As they parted ways, they each said goodbye.

"Hasta luego prima," Meredith said.

"Besos," Alicia replied.

Alicia turned left towards The Patchouli Mystical Tesoros Shop and Meredith crossed the street to Hannah's Tea House.

Chapter 3

Alicia's Patchouli Mystical Tesoros Shop had been the buzz of the town since she announced her latest creation. The witches and warlocks from the local and nearby covens were buying them sooner than she could make them.

Only those with magical capability knew the power of her *special* candles. One particular candle, Bright Eyes, allowed you to see into the immediate future. Not particularly useful to many, but for some that's all they needed. A few seconds into the future made a huge difference.

Alicia had created enough inventory to last her until the end of the season. On-line orders were plentiful, and a few surprises were in shop for the local witches and warlocks from her coven. Life was good. She had even decided to create a new collection that would help the earth witches. What amazed her the most was how quickly her inventory dwindled from the moment she flipped the shop sign to Open.

As she reached her shop at precisely seven-thirty on the third of October, it suddenly hit her, a sense of dread. Looking around she didn't notice anything out of the ordinary or anyone running away or hurt.

It was probably lack of sleep. She thought to herself, chucking it off to not having rested enough. Shrugging, she inserted the key to her shop, unlocked the door and entered.

Distracted she fumbled with her keys which she almost dropped to the floor. Just as she was about to walk across the room, she noticed a body. A dead body to be precise, right there in her shop.

No puede ser. This cannot be happening? Those were the first thoughts that crossed her mind. Not whether or not he needed help. She knew it, she had a sense of dread before she entered her shop, and sure enough here it was, a dead body. Alicia didn't have to inspect the corpse to know he was beyond help.

Then it dawned on her that someone had killed this man and it happened inside her own shop. Great!

Looking around she realized nothing seemed out of place, not even a forced entry. Wouldn't hey have entered the shop illegally to rob her? To take some of her inventory? But nothing seemed to have been disturbed. *Now, that's strange*, she thought to herself.

Knowing she had no choice; she took out her cell number and dialed the local sheriff's office.

"Wisterious Bay, where is your emergency?" the 911 operator asked.

"Hi... I... ah... want to report a crime," she stumbled with her words.

"Alicia? Alicia is that you?"

"Yes, Bertha. It's me. I need to report a murder," she tried her best to remain calm.

"Oh my. Where are you now?" Bertha asked.

"I'm at my shop. Can you please tell Sheriff McDonald to come out here?" she asked dreaded the thought of having to deal with him.

He was not keen on her becoming involved in any way shape or form in any mysteries or crimes in his town. That he had made abundantly clear over and over again.

They had history and not the loving kind. Alicia had solved several crimes in the past and had made him look rather foolish for not having solved the crime before she did. So, whenever a crime happened, she tried to stay out it. This time however, she had no choice. If a body appeared in her shop, she'd probably be the number one suspect and she couldn't let the Sheriff get the upper hand.

As Alicia waited for McDonald, she decided to light the two candles Gertrude had used before as they were the perfect combination to Zen the room. She needed to center herself. Taking several deep breaths, she said a silent prayer asking for protection and for light to be able to see clearly. *Necesito luz y protección.*

Taking a deep breath, she turned to the body to inspect it.

As she looked at his face, she realized it was Sam. Now she was more perplexed than ever. What was the town flirt doing in her shop?

23

Que hacia Sam aquí? What on earth would propel him to break in to my shop? All of these thoughts were swirling in her head at once.

Focusing her attention back to the body, she noted he had been stabbed. That was obvious from the knife protruding from his back. The knife had a very specific carving, the face of a moose.

Without touching it she realized it was one of the knives from her kitchen in the back of the shop. Great, she thought to herself. Now Sheriff McDonald had a reason to think she was involved. Inspecting his body, a bit more she didn't find anything else that stood out.

Just as she was leaning over the body, Sheriff McDonald entered the shop.

"Making sure he's really dead Alicia?" he asked as he approached the body.

Standing up, she glared at him before answering.

"No, as you well know I had nothing to do with this. I wouldn't hurt a fly," she replied.

"I don't know such a thing. All I know is that there's a dead man in your shop and when I walked in you were hovering over the body," he answered as he stood next to her.

Taking a deep breath, she ignored him.

"Step aside please," he demanded as he bent over to inspect the body.

Alicia walked away and stood behind the counter. She didn't want to be anywhere near him, and certainly not give him any more reason to think she might be the killer.

Soon, the shop was swarming with the remaining local officers. The Sherriff's department only had a total of six officers and that included McDonald. Murder is not common in these parts so next came the townspeople. Alicia knew the moment she called in the murder the gossip would spread like wild fire.

Through the front window, Alicia could see her cousin, her coven sisters including Laura, and some of the townspeople all staring and waiting to hear further news.

Sheriff McDonald turned to Alicia interrupting her thoughts.

"Tell me, when was the last time you saw Sam?" he asked Alicia as he took out his little black notebook. He was old school and preferred writing everything down by pencil.

"I think the last time was a few days ago. He and Dolores were having breakfast at The Cauldron Coffee Shop," she replied trying to think if that was the last time, she'd seen him.

"Did you exchange words?" he asked still writing in his notebook.

"What do you mean exchange words?" she needed to make sure she understood what he was asking before giving him an answer.

"Did you argue?" he asked rather impatiently, this time looking directly at her.

"No. Why would we argue? I hardly knew him or her for that matter. The only thing we did was exchange a good morning," she answered.

She knew better than to tell him she had seen him lurking around the alleyway a few times in the past. His response to her was he was taking a break from Dolores and that was the only place he could escape unnoticed. Alicia never said anything to him, but at the time it did seem odd that his spot to escape included her alleyway.

Just as she was about to say something, Deputy Donaldson came up to the Sheriff and whispered in his ear. Alicia tried to listen, but couldn't decipher what he was saying.

Sheriff McDonald looked at Alicia and instructed her to make sure she didn't leave town.

"I'll continue this interview later. Come by the station at two-o'clock this afternoon," he said and without waiting for a response walked outside with Deputy Donaldson.

The coroner, Ralph Henderson had just arrived and was working on examining the body. He loudly estimated on a time of death as he spoke to his assistant.

A short time later, Deputy Donaldson had returned and stood by the coroner before speaking.

"Anything specific to share?" Deputy Donaldson asked knowing the answer before he even asked the question.

"You know I can't give you an exact time of death. What I can tell you is that it appears, mind you, appears is the operative word, that the cause of death was a stab wound. However, I'll know better once I can do a thorough autopsy in the lab. Until then, I have nothing further to tell you Deputy," he looked up and replied.

Ralph went back to briefly examining the body and providing notes to his assistant. He then stood, removed his gloves and instructed the two men who had been waiting with the gurney to take to the body to his lab.

Alicia needed to wait a bit more until the entire shop was swept for prints. She thought it was a useless endeavor as there would be lots of prints. *It's a store*, *Por Dios,* she thought to herself. *Of course, it's going to have lots of prints.*

A bit exasperated she headed back to her kitchen when one of the officers stopped her.

"Alicia, I'm sorry but you can't go back there until we've checked and cleared the area," he stood his ground.

"Fine. I'll go back to the counter and wait until everyone is done," she turned around and whispered to herself *it's not like I have a choice*, as she headed back to the front of the shop.

It took a few more hours before everyone was done. Finally, Deputy Donaldson informed Alicia they had concluded with their preliminary investigation. He also reminded her not to forget to stop by the station later that afternoon to finish her interview with Sheriff McDonald.

"You know how he gets, especially when it concerns you. I don't know what it is, but you seem to bring out the worst in him," he said as he left the shop.

The moment Deputy Donaldson closed the door, Alicia collapsed face down on the counter. Immediately, the bell jingled as the door opened letting her know someone had entered. She didn't need to look up to know it was Meredith and a few of her friends.

"What happened?" Meredith was the first to speak.

Looking up she shrugged and thinking they wouldn't leave until she told them what she knew she put her finger up.

"Hold on before I tell you anything, which by the way is not much, I need to get something to drink. I'll be right back," she said as she headed to the back kitchen.

A few minutes later Alicia emerged looking a bit refreshed and holding a bottle of water.

"Alright ladies. I'll tell you what I know. After I left The Cauldron Coffee Shop, I came here to prepare the shop before opening as I had given Gertrude the day off to be with her visiting cousin," she informed the group.

"Gertrude has a cousin?" one of them asked looking at the others in the room.

"Yes, he showed up unexpectedly and it appears he might be here for a while," Meredith responded.

Before continuing, Alicia wondered if Gertrude's cousin showing up after years of not being in contact with her was more than a coincidence, interesting. She'd made a mental note of that idea for later.

"Anyway, after the coffee shop I came here to open the shop and the moment I walked inside there was Sam's body lying in the center of the room with a knife sticking out of his back," she stated solemnly.

"Wow, who could've killed him?" Meredith asked looking around hoping someone had some thoughts on the matter.

"I have no idea, but the fact that the knife was one of the ones from the back kitchen and the fact that I'm the one that found him and called in the crime has Sheriff McDonald salivating. Let's hope he doesn't arrest me for a crime I didn't commit," she stated shrugging.

Just then Laura walked into the shop. She had remained outside texting on her phone when everyone else entered.

"Are you alright?" she as she approached Alicia and hugged her.

"Yes, a little shaken up, but I'm fine," she replied as she attempted to smile.

"Well, we should do a cleansing. I'll contact the rest of the coven and ask them to come over as soon as possible so that when you open the shop later this afternoon any trace of Sam will be gone," Laura said as she turned around and walked to the far side of the room to make her phone calls.

The jingled again indicating someone else was entering the shop. This time it was Dolores who stormed into the shop wide eyed and screaming.

"You, you killed my Sam!" she screamed accusingly pointing her finger at Alicia.

"Dolores, I'm sorry for your loss," Alicia tried to keep calm.

"No! You're lying. You killed Sam! Everyone knows you were interested in him and because he didn't feel the same way about you, you killed him!" Dolores said now sobbing even more.

Shocked by the accusation, Alicia looked around the room shaking her head as they shrugged. Everyone remained silent.

"Dolores, I promise you, I had nothing to do with his death," Alicia tried to console her fruitlessly.

"This is all your fault!" She screamed even louder and then just as she had entered, she stormed right back out of the shop.

"Wow, what was that all about?" Meredith asked looking confused.

"I'm sure it was the shock of finding out that Sam was dead. She probably needs to blame someone and right now I'm the only one as he was in my shop. I should have asked her if she knew why he was here, but I'm sure I'll be able to do that once she's calmed down and realizes I had nothing to do with his murder," Alicia announced to everyone that was in the shop.

Laura approached the group while still on the phone.

"Several of the coven members are heading over now. They should be here shortly," Laura announced.

"Great. Thanks for taking care of that Laura," Alicia replied realizing at that moment that everyone that was in the shop knew about the coven. So, there was no need to do a spell to make them forget what they'd just overheard.

Before she knew it, The Patchouli Mystical Tesoros shop was surrounded by several of her coven members, all strategically placed throughout the shop swishing back and forth the sage and saying a prayer. They rest of the folks that had been in the shop stood in one corner. The coven members then gathered together in the center of the room and all held hands while Laura blessed the shop and wished Sam a peaceful transition into the afterlife.

When they were done, Alicia thanked everyone before they left. Soon only Meredith remained.

"We're alone. Que tu cres que sucedió? Tell me what you think really happened or at least what you know," Meredith asked as she took Alicia's hand.

"Well, this morning has been rather strange," Alicia told them. "I saw Laura having a heated conversation with someone as I mentioned already. Recently, I'd found Sam lurking in the alleyway. His excuse was that he was taking a reprieve from Dolores. Then when I stopped at the shop earlier this morning, Gertrude was here with her cousin. Which leads me to wonder if he knew Sam or maybe even had a reason to kill him. Oh, and then after our coffee meeting this morning, I came into the shop and that's when I found Sam dead. That's all I know," Alicia said sounding exhausted.

"Well, that's something alright. Wow! It's unbelievable that you found a body in your shop and that someone we may know could be the killer," Meredith stated nodding her head in disbelief.

"Puede ser. Could be, but I'm not sure yet. I am going to speak with my familiars to see if they can help," she answered.

"Good idea. If anyone can help it's those two," Meredith laughed.

Meredith was the only one who knew about her familiars. Felix, was a talking skeleton and Augustus, a banished reaper who came to life after dark.

"Speaking of Felix and Augustus, I need to get myself a cat or some animal so that the coven leaves me alone and stops telling me I need a familiar," Alicia sighed taking a deep breath.

"How about a gold fish?" Meredith laughed.

"Very funny. I'm serious. I don't want anyone outside us two ever finding out about them," She responded, always worried.

"Fine. You can't take a joke, she said. "No worries, we'll figure something out, but I think you're right, the best solution would be to get a cat," Meredith stated.

"Puede ser. Could be as Haydee my neighbor, has a cat that just had kittens. I'll go over later today and ask if there are any left. Will you help me buy food and everything else I'll need if I get the kitten?" Alicia asked.

"Perfecto, it'll be fun and we'll even come up with a cool name," Meredith smiled.

"It's a deal. Go on now. Vamos I'll be fine. I need to clean up a bit before I can open the shop," Alicia said as she looked at her apple watch and ushered her prima to the door.

"I have less than an hour," she said.

"If you need anything, I'll be just a few doors down. Hablamos pronto. Besos prima," she replied as she hugged and kissed Alicia on her way out. "Talk later."

After she had left, Alicia rubbed her temples. Taking a deep breath, she looked around and without any more delays, got to work. By the time she turned the sign to Open, she had cleaned up the shop, replenished the candles that needed restoking, and placed the pumpkin bread and the coffee pot on the makeshift table.

Shortly after ten o'clock, the bell jingled as the door opened and the first customer entered. After that, it was nonstop until she turned the sign to Closed later that afternoon. Alicia cleaned up the makeshift coffee table taking everything to the kitchen. She threw away the garbage with the paper plates and coffee cups. Then she scrubbed the table, cleaned the coffee pot, and blew out all of the candles. She was exhausted.

Before she left, she made sure the back door that led to the alleyway was locked, then returned to the front of the shop and walked out and locked the door behind her thinking at the time that maybe it was time to install some security.

Alicia walked next door to her neighbor's house before she went home to see about the kitten.

Knocking, she waited.

"Who is it?" came the voice from behind the door.

"Hi, it's Alicia. Sorry to bother you, I'm here to inquire about your kittens?" she asked.

Opening the door, Haydee smiled.

"Come on in my dear," she smiled as she opened the door wider.

Haydee was over seventy years old. Her exact age was unknown as she gave out a different birth year anytime anyone she was asked about her age.

"I'm sorry to bother you. I just wanted to see if you still had any kittens left. I'm thinking of getting a cat and wanted to check with you first if that's alright?" Alicia asked.

"Yes, as a matter of fact I have two kittens left. A female and a male. Both are jet black and are ready to be taken if you want either of them or both of them. Do you want to see them?" she asked as she closed the door behind her.

"That would be wonderful," Alicia smiled as she followed Haydee to the back area of the house.

Haydee had set up a room dedicated specifically for the cats with scratching pads, litter boxes, and toys. Alicia noticed that one of the kittens just sat in the back of the room and didn't move. The other one raced around the room playing with one of the toys.

For some reason Alicia was drawn to the one kitten in the corner. Something about it drew her in as it looked up and meowed at her. Jet black with piercing eyes that seemed to be looking directly into your soul.

"I'll take the one in the corner," Alicia said out loud without thinking.

"Are you sure that's the one you want?" Haydee asked. "It doesn't really move around too much. It's healthy, I've had all of the kittens checked. There's nothing wrong with her, it's just that she chooses to spend her time laying around the room and never really interacted with any of her siblings," she stated smiling at Alicia.

"Yes, that's perfect. Let me ask you something, can this be an outside cat or does it have to be inside at all times?" Alicia asked.

"From what I've notice about this one, I don't think you have to worry if you decide to make her an outside cat. She seems to have a mind of her own and is already very independent. May I suggest you let her choose?" Haydee asked with a twinkle in her eye.

Let her choose? Alicia thought to herself.

Chapter 4

Sure enough, the female kitten continued to meow at Alicia until she picked her up. She then purred making Alicia giggle.

Setting the kitten down, Alicia thanked Haydee and told her she'd let her know of her decision. Although she had already made up her mind, she didn't want to come across as desperate. Besides, tonight all she had wanted to do was take a long bath, and then wait until her familiars came to life, so that she could pick their brains. Tomorrow would be another day and Alicia had a feeling this kitten would be hers soon.

Before she left, Haydee agreed to hold on to her new kitten until Alicia was able to buy everything she needed for the house.

Alicia thanked her and walked next door to her own house. As she walked inside, she took her cell phone out of her pocket and dialed Meredith's number.

"Hey prima, everything alright?" Meredith asked.

"Yes, sorry I didn't mean to alarm you. I was just calling to let you know that I decided to get a kitten. I stopped by Haydee's house and she had two left from the litter. One in particular was drawn to me. She's keeping her until I buy everything, I need to bring her home. So, will you go with me tomorrow to buy the essentials and also help me give her a name?" Alicia asked.

"Of course. I can't wait to meet the new addition to your family," Meredith said. "This will be good, you'll see. Have you decided if it's going to be an outside cat or indoor cat?" Meredith inquired.

"Que cómica. Funny you should ask. Haydee suggested I let the cat decide," Alicia laughed.

"Oh my, that's too funny. Well, I can lend you one of the litter boxes I have in storage until you have decided. That way you don't have to purchase one if you don't need it," she suggested.

"Gracias. That would be wonderful. Since tomorrow is Saturday, can we go shopping early? Let's say around ten in the morning?" Alicia asked.

"Sure, stop by the house. I'll have coffee and scones waiting, and then we can head out together," Meredith suggested.

"Perfecto prima. See you tomorrow morning. Good night," Alicia replied and placed the phone down.

Now that that was settled, she headed to the bathroom. She turned on the water poured in some salt bath crystals, and waited until it was just the right temperature. She removed her clothing and placed them in her hamper. Slowly she entered the tub and as she emerged her body she began to relax.

After spending more time than she realized, she stood showered off the excess soap. Alicia had lost track of time thinking about Sam and the fact that there was a killer in her own town of Wisterious Bay. Taking a deep breath, she dried herself off. Grabbing the robe behind the door she secured the tie around her waist and went towards the kitchen to make dinner.

She decided she wanted something light, so she prepared a salad, a turkey burger, and cauliflower mash potato. As she finished her meal, she heard noises coming from the basement.

"Hi, guys, I'm up here," she called out to Felix and Augustus.

Felix couldn't help himself and made clanking noises as his feet hit each step. Augustus made no noise which at first was creepy. Now, she was used to both of them.

"What's cooking?" Felix, the humorous one, clanked his mouth as he spoke.

He really didn't speak per se, as he didn't have any vocal cords. But he did seem to be able to hold a conversation. One day she'd ask him how he did that, but for now she had other pressing matters.

"I've had a heck of a day. Let me tell you," Alicia replied.

"What happened?" Augustus said with his voice deep and sultry voice.

"This morning I found Sam dead in my shop. To make matters worse he had one of the knives from the back kitchen sticking out of his back," she answered them looking deflated.

"Oh yeah, I can see it was his time," Augustus answered.

"Couldn't you have warned me?" Alicia asked not believing what was saying.

Augustus shook his head before answering her.

"You know I have been relieved of my reaper duties. So, no I couldn't tell you beforehand. Sorry," he replied.

"Felix, do you know anything about Sam or his death that can help me figure out what happened to him and most importantly who killed him?" she asked anxiously.

"Nope," Felix said. "Nothing is coming through," he nodded.

"I figured as much, but it never hurts to ask," Alicia looked from one to the other before continuing.

"I'm going to need you both to help out on this one. Since the body was found in the shop you know Sheriff McDonald will find every reason to charge me with the murder. So, let's get sleuthing," she said.

They nodded in unison.

"By the way, you know how the coven has been harassing me to get a familiar? Since they don't know about either of you, I've decided to get a kitten. According to everyone outside this house that will be my familiar. This is the only way to appease them and not risk having you both exposed," she paused and waited for a reaction.

All at once Felix started clattering and Augustus breathed heavily. This was their way of letting her know they weren't impressed.

"Guys. I have no choice. It's either that or someone will eventually find out about you. You, Augustus, know very well you must remain in hiding if you don't want them coming and taking you away. And, you

Felix, it's not natural to have a talking skeleton. I don't want anything to happen to either of you. So, please can you both cooperate?" she asked.

This was a recurring discussion. Every few months they'd become restless and she had to reel them in by reminding them how prudent it was that they remained hidden and known only to her and her cousin Meredith.

"Yes, we'll behave," Augustus answered for both of them rather solemnly.

"Thank you," she replied.

Her nervousness about telling them her idea of the new kitten had evaporated. Not only was she happy it had gone well, but it was impossible to be anxious when she was surrounded by such wonderful and accepting colorful familiars.

Feeling good about her decision, she cleaned up after herself and then grabbed a pad and pencil.

The obvious question was, who would want Same dead? Returning to the dining room table she wrote out a list of possible suspects. Then she realized she didn't really know him. So, she switched it up and wrote; who was Sam?

What she did know, was he and Dolores had arrived in town several years back. They were in their late sixties and both said they had been retired for a few years. As far as Alicia could remember no one had a problem with Sam. As a matter of fact, the one that had a short temper was Dolores.

So, the first name she wrote down was obviously Dolores. Then she drew a blank. Alicia figured she needed to do some more research and a bit of sleuthing before she could determine what other suspects there were if any at all.

Not having much luck in digging up potential suspects, she decided to retire early.

The next morning Alicia woke early ready to tackle a new day. After getting her much needed morning coffee, she showered and dressed.

She decided to go to the shop early. There wasn't really a reason, she just wanted to make sure there wasn't another body lying in the center of the room. As she exhaled, she hadn't realized she had been holding her breath. Satisfied, she smiled.

Spur of the moment, she decided to stop at The Cauldron Coffee Shop. So, she sent Meredith a text.

Change of plans, meet me at the Cauldron.

When she opened the door a whiff of air pushed her in, ever so slightly right into the arms of Valentino.

"Wow. Are you alright?" He said smiling as he held her.

"Uh, yes. Sorry. I don't know what happened," she stepped back, as her face grew warm. She tried to avoid eye contact, but she couldn't help herself.

Valentino chuckled.

"No problem, but we really do need to stop meeting this way," he now was grinning.

"So... have you found a place to stay yet?" she asked stumbling her words.

What was the matter with her, she thought to herself.

No matter how much she tried, the few times she'd been around Valentino, she seemed to lose all sense of control and fumbled her words like a high school girl.

"I have several places lined up. Hopefully, I'll find something suitable unless you have space in your house?" he winked.

Now Alicia was truly blushing.

"Well," she didn't finish the sentence.

"I didn't mean to put you on the spot. Sorry. No worries, I was only kidding," he chuckled.

Alicia was relieved. There was no way she could have Valentino stay at her house. It wasn't a matter of not wanting him to stay at her house. It was the fact that she had two unorthodox familiars and well, truth be told, he was just too distracting.

"Of course. Anyway, good luck on your house hunting," she said as stepped around him.

When she looked around, she found Meredith sitting at a table wearing a smile from ear to ear.

"Well, well. I see you are being friendly to our new guest," she laughed.

"Very funny. What is it about him that has me in knots?" she whined.

"Oh please," Meredith said. "The sparks between you two are so strong they could light up the sky.

Alicia glanced back just as Valentino turned around. Sparks definitely flew.

Turning back around she took a deep breath and ignored her cousin's comment.

"So, thank you for meeting me here," Alicia said.

"What's going on and how are you holding up?" Meredith asked.

"Actually, quite well. Felix and Augustus complained a bit of course, but in the end, they agreed it was the best solution. They were even making plans when I went to bed. You can imagine, it'll be quite interesting once the kitten is officially part of the family," she replied.

"The fun part now is going shopping and picking a name. Any ideas on a female name?" Meredith asked.

"No idea whatsoever. That's where hopefully you come in, because if it's left to me, I'll call it Kitty," Alicia laughed.

"Sure. Let me think of a few names and I'll let you know by the time you're ready to pick her up today," Meredith responded.

Alicia looked around the coffee shop and noticed several people reading the morning newspaper. Not everyone, but some were looking at her. Alicia wondered if they thought she may have had something to do with Sam's death. She needed to clear up this murder as quickly as possible.

Turning back to Meredith she whispered.

"I need to find out what really happened to Sam soon. People are going to start pointing fingers and I don't want McDonald to have any ammunition. The problem is that I realized that I didn't know Sam except for the fact that he and Dolores were an item and they both said they were retired," Alicia said.

"Dolores has her hair and nails done at the Salon usually on the same day I'm there. We've gotten to chat a bit," she replied.

"Oh, that's good. Tell me anything you can about either of them," Alicia encouraged her.

Meredith told her what she did know as Alicia listened intently.

"There's something else I wanted to tell you," Alicia sounded rather mysteriously.

"What?" Meredith leaned in closer.

"I have a date..."

"Wait! What? You have a date? I want to know everything." Meredith now sounded excited.

Laughing Alicia spoke.

"Prima, you have to give me a chance to tell you," She laughed.

"Por dios. Fine. Go tell me," Meredith chuckled knowing she needed to be patient if she wanted to find out about Alicia's upcoming mysterious date.

"Valentino, Gertrude's cousin asked me out on a date," Alicia finally said.

"That's wonderful prima! I'm so happy for you. When is the big day?" she asked.

"We haven't finalized a date yet. The reason I'm bringing it up is to ask you if I should actually go on this date? It's been so long I've been out with a man, I'm not certain I have the time," she said looking directly at Meredith.

"Well, if your blushing is any indication of how you feel, then I'd say go out on a date with Valentino," Meredith smiled.

Taking a deep breath, Alicia looked at Meredith and told her she'd think about it. Who was she kidding, there was no question about it, Alicia would go out on a date with Valentino.

When they were done, they paid their bills and headed out. The stores would be opening soon so they decided to walk around Main Street until then. Gertrude would be covering the shop, so that gave Alicia open reign to go shopping without having to worry about having to go to the shop.

"Good morning, Alicia, Meredith," a voice interrupted her thoughts.

"Haydee, buenos días," Alicia smiled and leaned in to hug her. Meredith did the same.

"Meredith and I are going to pick up somethings and then we were going to give you a call to see at what time I could stop by to pick up the kitten," she warmly touched her arm as she smiled.

"Yes, the kitten in the corner. I know exactly which one you're talking about. That's wonderful news. You'll be very happy, I'm certain. She's full of surprises," Haydee smiled.

"Thank you, I agree. By the way, I'm trying to figure out who could've wanted Sam dead. Do you think you'd be willing to speak to me about him?" she asked.

"I don't know too much about Sam, but if I can help in anyway, you can count on me. Stop by any time after three o'clock, no need to call first," Haydee replied.

"Perfecto. See you then," she answered.

They said their goodbyes and each continued to their final destination.

Chapter 5

After Alicia had purchased all the things she needed for her new kitten, she and Meredith dropped off the packages at the shop and headed to lunch.

Lunch at Hannah's Tea House was always crowded. Meredith excused herself and went to the back to check on her staff. This gave Alicia an opportunity to see if anyone was talking about Sam.

As Alicia sat, she noticed Dolores was sitting two tables away. She was crying and as she dabbed her eyes with a handkerchief, she leaned in and whispered. Dolores saw her staring and, in a huff, turned away.

"I don't understand why Dolores thinks I'm to blame for Sam's murder?" Alicia asked Meredith after she returned.

"Don't mind her, she's just still in shock about what happened. It hasn't even been more than twenty-four hours since he was murdered. She needs to blame someone until the killer is found and you just happen to be the easiest target," Meredith replied.

"I know, but still, it bothers me that she thinks I could be a killer," Alicia asked.

"We'll figure it out. For now, let's focus on lunch," Meredith said trying to distract Alicia even if just for a moment.

"Yes, prima. That's a good idea. I need to eat, so tell me about your specials today. We'll tackle Same while we eat," Alicia replied.

"Good idea. Today's special made especially for you. Cuban sandwich with a flan on the side. It'll compliment the tea of the day, Tilo," she smiled.

"Perfecto. Gracias," Alicia replied as she squeezed Meredith's hand.

"This is exactly what I needed," Alicia sighed.

After they ordered, Alicia looked around and noticed a few people looking her way. She just smiled and nodded. Trying not to roll her eyes she closed them instead and then in her mind rolled her eyes. *Por Dios*, she thought to herself.

"Well, I've been thinking of names for your kitten and this is what I have so far. Mind you, I'm just throwing out names for consideration. There's Rosalinda, Twinkle, Berta, and Zoraida," Meredith said.

"Oh, I like them all," she laughed.

"You need to pick one silly or we can continue to brainstorm," Meredith chuckled.

"Alright, alright. How about Zoraida? I like the way it sounds," Alicia said as she closed her eyes and repeated the name several times in her mind.

"Are you sure?" Meredith asked.

"Yes, I love it! Zoraida it is," Alicia said as she clapped her hands.

"Well, then this has been a successful adventure," Meredith smiled.

When Alicia took a bite from her sandwich, she moaned.

"Que rico!" she smiled and nodded at Meredith.

Laughing she told her she knew it would be a hit. Looking around the tea house she noticed a lot of the patrons had ordered the same thing.

"It seems you're not the only one who is enjoying a Cuban sandwich," she boasted.

"Well, they better or I'll put a hex on them," Alicia laughed.

"Gracias prima," Meredith responded warmly.

"Thank you for what, prima?" Alicia asked.

"Just for being you," Meredith said letting her prima know how she felt.

"By the way when did we start calling each other prima instead of cuz?" Alicia asked.

"No idea, but you know what I like prima better. So, no more cuz. It sounds weird anyway," Meredith replied.

"Sounds like a plan, prima," Alicia said and stretched out her hand.

Meredith shaking her hand tightly proclaimed, prima it is.

When they were done Alicia said she was going home to get the house ready for the new arrival and asked Meredith to stop by later that evening to meet Zoraida.

"Hay si, yes," Meredith clapped her hands.

"By the way lunch is on me," Meredith said as she blocked Alicia's hand from retrieving her money.

"Gracias, prima," Alicia smiled.

They stood hugged and parted ways.

Alicia decided to head back to the shop and work on her candles. In the basement of the shop, she had discovered when she first moved in a room that spanned the size of the room upstairs. Enough space to put her tables, a small stove, microwave and plenty of shelves. Everything she needed to make her candles was right there at arms' length. Her sacred witch recipe book she kept under lock and key hidden behind a false wall.

Besides her traditional Patchouli candle, she had created a few new ones lately that she wanted to try out on her customers. Besides she needed to make more mostly because she wanted to make sure she had enough inventory to last her until the end of October.

So, she pulled out her witch recipe book, wrote down three new names and their ingredients, and got to work

By late afternoon, Alicia was ready to head home. Before she left, she made a note and added Hearts Desire, Double Toil, and Dash Away to her inventory list. She then locked her recipe book once again behind lock and key and pushed the false wall back into place. Anyone who entered the basement would see a small room with several boxes stacked up against the wall on the far end of the room. No one would suspect that behind the bookshelf was an entirely different room.

Alicia, was so excited to pick up her new kitten that she almost forgot her packages. *Hay Dios Mio,* she thought to herself. She double checked everything was secure in the shop and grabbed her packages before walking out the door. Looking around to make sure no one was noticing her, she did a protection spell, locked the door and headed home.

She arrived at her house in no time, dropped off her packages and set everything in place for her new arrival. Her familiars hadn't awakened yet so she had some time before they'd meet Zoraida.

Satisfied everything was set-up, she walked next door.

Haydee opened the door before Alicia had a chance to knock.

"How is it you always know I'm here before I can knock?" Alicia chuckled.

"Oh, you know it's my sixth sense," she smiled.

If Alicia didn't know any better, she'd say, Haydee was psychic. But she'd never made any indication. *She probably noticed me from her window, that was it. That explains it*, she thought to herself.

"Come on in, your kitten is ready to go," she said as she opened the door further.

"Wonderful. I can't wait to bring her home," Alicia replied following her to the back room.

"Have you named her yet?" Haydee asked as she turned around and looked directly at Alicia.

"Yes, I've decided on naming her Zoraida," Alicia responded gazing into her eyes to see how she'd respond.

"Zoraida," Haydee repeated the name out loud.

"I like it. What do you think?" She asked the kitten as she picked her up from the playpen.

Looking at Alicia, Haydee smiled.

"She likes her new name. Zoraida is perfect," Haydee smiled as she handed the kitten to Alicia.

Looking into the kitten's piercing blue gray eyes, Alicia spoke.

"Hi Zoraida, I hope you'll be happy living in my house. I promise to take care of you and love you," she smiled as she cuddled her new kitten.

The cat purred and Alicia could've sworn she nodded.

Ridiculous, cats can't talk, she thought to herself.

That being settled Haydee asked Alicia if she'd like to sit.

"My dear, would you like a cafecito. Ever since you taught me how to make it, that's all I drink," Haydee chuckled.

"Yes, that would be wonderful," Alicia replied as picked up the kitten and placed her on her lap. She then scratched her on the side of her face until she settled on Alicia's lap and purred.

"I'll make some now," Haydee said as she headed to the kitchen. Make yourself at home and I'll be back in a jiffy," she stated.

For the next few minutes Alicia stroked Zoraida making her purr even more.

"Here we go," Haydee said when she returned with a tray.

Setting it down she asked Alicia if she wanted any sugar or milk.

"No, if it already has sugar. I don't need anymore and I like my cafecito without any additional sugar or milk. Thanks," Alicia replied.

As Haydee served her cafecito she asked Alicia what she wanted to know about Sam?

"I was hoping you could tell me anything you know or if you even have any idea who could've killed him?" She inquired.

"Who killed him no, but I can tell you what I know about him and Dolores," she replied.

Alicia took out her notebook and started to write. By the time Haydee had finished Alicia had two full pages of notes. She learned that Sam and Dolores had previously lived in Wisterious Bay when they were younger. They used to frequent the area with their families during the summer. As they got older, they parted ways until they ran into each other again.

The last few years after they retired, they realized they were bored and needed to find something to keep them occupied. So, they started to dabble in real estate. They now are the number one Realtors in Wisterious Bay. As far as Haydee knew, Sam and Dolores didn't have any family of their own or if they did, they never mentioned them.

Once a year they opened their home and invited the townspeople. Everyone knew the reason was because they wanted their business, but almost everyone accepted the invitation mainly for the free food and drinks.

They had expanded their services and were now buying rundown homes, restoring them and adding them to their Airbnb inventory.

"Maybe one of the guests killed him? But still, that doesn't explain why he was in the shop after hours and how did he get in?" She said out loud.

"That's a possibility. We have seen lately an influx of tourists come into the area and I've heard them saying they were staying in one of Dolores' properties," Haydee replied.

"Thank you. This has been helpful," Alicia stated as she stood up.

Haydee brought over the travel bag Alicia had brought over when she arrived. Opening up the top flap for her, Alicia placed Zoraida inside and closed the zipper.

"Un placer," Haydee tried saying you're welcome in Spanish.

"That's perfect Haydee. You're picking up the language quite nicely," she smiled.

"It's so much fun. Soon I'll be able to converse with you and Meredith like a pro," Haydee laughed.

"Oh, count on it!" Alicia chuckled.

As Alicia left, she thought about a spell she'd learned from her mother. She couldn't believe she'd previously forgotten it.

When she got home, she opened up the travel bag and took out Zoraida. She placed her in a mini playpen she had set-up in the main living room. She then went searched amongst her mother's belongings and sure enough there it was in her personal spell book. The Truth Revealing Spell.

Knowing she still had time before her familiars woke up, she gathered all the ingredients and headed to her lab.

"Now, you stay right there Zoraida. I know Haydee fed you earlier so you should be alright for a bit while I tend to something important," Alicia said as she petted Zoraida.

Once she gathered all the ingredients, she needed she left her house quickly and headed to her shop. Unlocking the door, she turned on the light briefly. She just needed to make sure there were no bodies in her shop. She then locked the door behind her and turned off the light. With the light from her cell, she walked over to the back of the shop and went into her lab. Setting the candle in a safe place, and lighting it, she read from the book.

Necesito saber la verdad,

I seek the truth and I will not rest,

At my behest, a mi instancia, you will be revealed to me,

With this light I seek the truth.

Vamos a ver que pasa ahora, Alicia thought to herself. Something or someone would be bound to be revealed soon enough. In the meantime, she'd do her sleuthing the old way. First stop, would be the hair salon precisely when Dolores had her appointment. She'd call Meredith in the morning to find out when the next time she was going to have her nails done and she'd accompany her to the appointment, she made a mental note to herself.

On her way home earlier, she had thought about what her customers liked best and was happy that she had worked on several new candles. She was certain they would fly off the shelves. She contemplated consulting Laura about what she was planning on doing. It couldn't hurt to bring in the coven to assist. Just then, she decided since there was a meeting coming up in the next couple of days, she'd take that opportunity to make an announcement.

At some point, Alicia looked at her watch and noticed she had had spent more time at the lab than initially intended and now she had less than an hour left before Felix and Augustus made their presence known. She put everything away, turned off all the lights from the lab, went to the front door, looked around and satisfied everything was fine, she opened the door. She closed it behind her, locked it and hurried home.

The moment she walked in the door she went straight to where she had left Zoraida. Taking a deep breath, she was happy to see the kitten was bundled up in a corner sleeping. As she approached the playpen, Zoraida opened one eye and meowed.

"I'm so sorry for leaving you alone. It's just that I needed to do this one thing and it couldn't wait. I'm here now, so let's go into the kitchen and see what goodies there are for you," Alicia said as she picked up Zoraida and stroked her fur.

Zoraida purred.

Smiling, Alicia walked towards the kitchen. There she set the kitten down on the floor and grabbed some of the dry food. She set some in Zoraida's bowl and waited until she had finished eating. She then picked her up and walked around the house. Alicia introduced Zoraida to the different rooms in the house, the crawl spaces, and even pointed towards the basement, telling her this is where her familiars rested during the day.

"You'll meet them soon enough. I hope you'll like them as much as hopefully they'll like you. For the most part Felix likes everyone, Augustus, well he's another matter. But don't you worry, I'll make sure they leave you alone," she said to Zoraida as the kitten looked up at Alicia.

"I hope you understand me, because I want to make sure you feel welcomed in my home," she said as she stroked Zoraida.

Zoraida purred and nodded.

If I didn't know any better, I'd say, she nodded. That's impossible, it's just my imagination. Although, how fun would it be if she too could communicate with me and my familiars, she thought to herself as she continued to stroke Zoraida.

Alicia heard it first, the clatter of bones coming up the stairs. From Zoraida's reaction she too heard the clatter. Her ears stood up and she looked from Alicia towards the noise and back again.

"Hola Felix. Hola Augustus," Alicia called out as they both appeared in the family room.

She had been holding Zoraida and watched as they slowly approached. It seemed as if there was not going to be a problem because as they neared Alicia, Zoraida began to meow and purr. Astonished, Alicia just watched as it appeared they had a conversation going. At one point, Felix's teeth clatter and he tilted his head back as if he was laughing.

"Interesante. Guess you guys hit it off?" She asked the group.

Felix clapped his hands together, Augustus stomped his scythe, and Zoraida purred.

Chapter 6

The next morning Alicia woke up earlier than usual. She had a dream where the motive behind Sam's death was revealed. But try as she did, she couldn't remember what it was. Frustrated, she got out of bed, showered, and headed to the kitchen to make a hearty breakfast. Zoraida followed. She placed some food in her bowl and once she'd done eating, she picked her up and took her to the guest room she had set up for her. It had a scratching pad, a litter box, and several toys to keep her busy while she was away.

Today promised to be a very busy day and Alicia wasn't sure if she'd have time for lunch.

On the way into the shop, she called Meredith to find out when her next appointment at the salon was and to see if she could tag along.

"Mañana temprano. I'll call and add you for a pedicure so that you're there at the same time and it won't look suspicious," Meredith answered.

"Gracias," Alicia replied and promised to talk to her later.

By the time she arrived at The Patchouli Mystical Tesoros Shop, she saw Gertrude through the window lighting the candles and plugging in the streamed lights she had all around the walls of the shop.

"Good morning," Alicia said as she walked in.

"Good morning to you," Gertrude replied with a smile. "I'm glad you're here. I forgot something at home and I wanted to go get it before the crowds arrive. Would that be alright?" She asked.

"Of course. Go on, see you in a bit," Alicia shushed her out the door.

While Gertrude was gone, Alicia turned on the coffee machine and prepared the makeshift table out in the shop for customers. Today she added a tea kettle with some pumpkin spicy chai, which was perfect for this time of year.

Before she knew it, Gertrude had returned.

Turning around she smiled as she heard the jingle of the door and Gertrude walked in with a box.

"What do we have here?" Alicia asked, pointing to the box.

"I brought some homemade cookies for our customers," Gertrude smiled.

"Did you bring the pumpkin spice cookies? The one whose recipe you refuse to share, those cookies?" Alicia asked.

Gertrude just laughed.

"Come on, I'll let you have one," she chuckled as she walked to the back of the shop and placed them on the kitchen table.

"Yummy. I just started the coffee," Alicia replied.

"I can't seem to get past the fact that someone killed Sam and most of all that it happened right out there," Alicia stated pointing towards the door.

"I know, it's tragic. I can't imagine who would've done such a thing. And, to think I dated him back when he first lived here," Gertrude responded as she shook her head.

"Wait what? You dated Same? You never mentioned that to me?" Alicia asked now more interested than ever to find out more.

"Nothing really to tell. We didn't end it on good terms. He went his way, I stayed and I hadn't seen him again until he showed up in town with Dolores," Gertrude replied in disgust.

"I take it you don't like Dolores? Or is it Sam you dislike?" Alicia asked.

"I don't know what you're talking about. Anyway, I'm so happy because Valentino found a place. He's definitely staying temporarily. I'm looking forward to him spending time here in Wisterious Bay," she smiled.

That was interesting, Alicia thought to herself, but didn't pursue it. It was obvious that Gertrude didn't want to talk about Sam. She'd approach the subject again at another time. Figured it was time to change the subject.

"That's wonderful. So, where will he be renting?" Alicia asked the question.

"He's actually renting the Henderson house," Gertrude replied.

"You mean the Henderson house? The one next door to me?" she gasped and starting coughing.

"What's wrong Alicia? Are you alright?" Gertrude sounded alarmed.

"Sorry, yes I, I tried to swallow at the same time as I took a breath and..." she said as she took a deep breath.

"Here let me get you some water," Gertrude said.

Next door? That can't be. Just knowing he's next door is going to drive me crazy. That man is... she thought to herself as she let her thoughts trail away.

"Here. Drink some water," Gertrude said as she handed Alicia a glass.

"Thank you," Alicia drank.

Gertrude cleared her throat before speaking.

"So, I wanted to let you know that I have some ideas for the shop if you have time this morning to chat?" Gertrude sounded excited.

"Sure. Let me just set up these breads I picked up this morning and take the coffee maker out there along with some of your yummy cookies, and we can talk until it's time to open," Alicia said as she stood and exited her kitchen.

A few minutes later, after checking that all was set, she turned to Gertrude.

"Alright, let's hear it," she smiled.

"Well, you know how the town is big on festivities. I was thinking of doing a raffle to name your next candle. Maybe even give a hint as to one of the ingredients in your recipe?" Gertrude asked.

"I like the idea of a contest. However, I'm not so sure giving just one ingredient would make the difference, but I can think about it. It could be instead of an actual ingredient, the process or something similar," Alicia answered why pondering the options.

"We need the recipe. If you're willing to share with me, I promise not to let anyone know I have a copy. It'll be our secret," Gertrude prodded.

"Well, that's going to be difficult. It's a family recipe and no one outside my mother's side of the family has ever let anyone know the full recipe. But maybe it's time to share some of the ingredients. I'll think about it some more," Alicia replied knowing quite well she'd never share that recipe with anyone, no matter how much she trusted them to keep it a secret.

"I understand. In the meantime, I'll work on the sign to put up and if we decide to go for it at least it's already done. Maybe the prize can be a year's worth of the candle in small sample sizes, almost like a travel size portion," Gertrude thought out loud.

"I like it. Yes, work on the sign and I'll let you know later if it's doable," Alicia smiled.

She liked the idea of bringing more customers to the shop and holding a raffle always worked. They could even do the actual raffle during the week of Halloween when the town is full of tourist. Giving up even one of the ingredients, well, that was completely out of the question.

When it was time to turn the sign to open Alicia had thought of another idea, but kept it to herself until she could formulate a plan.

By the time lunch came around, Alicia had been so busy she hadn't even had a chance to catch her breath.

Alicia looked up when the door opened and the bells jingled. She held her breath before she grew dizzy. She hadn't even realized she had done that until she almost lost her balance. Luckily no one noticed.

"Good afternoon," Valentino said as he entered the shop.

"Well, hello there," Meredith coquettishly said as she had followed him into Patchouli's.

Turning around Valentino grinned.

"I don't think we've had the pleasure. I'm Valentino Perez, Gertrude's cousin," he said as he took her hand and kissed it.

Meredith giggled. Alicia rolled her eyes.

"And you, how have you been?" he asked as he addressed Alicia.

Now, she was annoyed that he was flirting with her cousin.

"Fine," she answered curtly.

"Glad to hear it," he stared at her intently.

Her stomach did a turn and she flushed.

"Hey, what brings you here?" Gertrude asked as she walked out of the back room.

"I decided to buy some candles for the house," he replied as he kept his eyes on Alicia.

Alicia's temperature rose and her blushing was not going away. Meredith realized what was happening and intervened.

"So, I heard you're renting locally?" She asked looking from him to Alicia back to him.

Taking his eyes off of Alicia, he turned towards Meredith and replied.

"Yes, I've rented the Henderson house for an indefinite stay. I heard this is the place to get the best candles and scents. So, I thought I'd give it a try," he replied with a smile.

"Absolutely, my cousin has the best shop in town and the most amazing candles," she answered him thinking if he only knew they were magical.

"Prima, why don't you show Valentino your latest creations?" she encouraged Alicia knowing quite well she'd never hear the end of it once he was gone.

"Aww, well..."

Before she could finish her sentence Gertrude came to the rescue.

"Let me. Come this way prima. We have the perfect candles for the house, trust me," she said as she dragged him to the other side of the shop.

Meredith got closer to Alicia and whispered.

"What was that all about?" Meredith said.

You could have sliced the tension and hormones with a knife and probably not even made a dent.

"I don't know what you're talking about," Alicia whispered trying to avoid looking at him.

"We'll discuss this later. I've embarrassed you enough for one day. If you're really too blind to see it, I'm just letting you know that there was something going on there and soon if you don't acknowledge it, it'll come back to bite you," Meredith laughed as she said goodbye to everyone and walked out the door.

As Gertrude was ringing up the candles Valentino was purchasing, she read each label out loud in her mind; Protection, Love Burst, Truth Be Told, Believer, and the house special, Patchouli Galore.

Interesting combination of candles, she thought to herself as he took out his credit card to pay.

Making eye contact again, Alicia felt the heat rising. Trying to act natural she smiled, but it came across as a distorted facial expression.

"Are you alright Alicia?" Valentino asked with a twinkle in his eye.

"Y-y-yes," she stammered. "Why do you ask?"

"You just seem to be, I don't know in pain?" He tried not to chuckle.

"I'm fine!" She huffed.

Gertrude, still not realizing there was something going on between them interrupted.

"You're all set," she said as she handed Valentino the bag of candles.

"Thank you," he replied to her.

"Have a wonderful day, Alicia," he said as he lingered just a little longer than necessary.

"Hope to see you again soon," and with that he turned around and walked out the door.

Again, she didn't realize she'd been holding her breath until Gertrude nudged her.

"Earth to Alicia. Did you not hear anything I said?" she asked.

Letting out a deep breath, she briefly closed her eyes and then faced Gertrude.

"Yes, I'm sorry I was just thinking about Sam," she replied trying not to make it obvious that she'd been affected by Valentino's presence.

"Oh, I understand. Although you have to realize there's nothing you can do about it. I'm sure Sheriff McDonald will figure out what happened to him soon enough. Don't make trouble for yourself," she warned Alicia.

"But you know that he will probably blame the wrong person, namely me," she sounded deflated.

"Nonsense. He'll figure it out. Besides I wouldn't want to see you in any danger. There's a killer out there and that puts anyone looking into the murder in his or her path," Gertrude countered.

"I guess you're right," she replied even though she disagreed with Gertrude's assessment of Sheriff McDonald. Alicia wasn't so sure he'd solve the crime any sooner than she could by investigating it herself.

Alicia knew that if left to him alone he'd arrest the wrong person and she couldn't let that happen. What actually had her head spinning was the fact that she felt now that she needed to add Gertrude to her suspect list.

It was evident, there was more to the story of her and Sam, and if she dug deeper maybe she'd find out what really happened to them and why she had the nagging sensation that Gertrude hated Sam. Maybe hatred was a strong word. She needed to think about that further.

Chapter 7

Two days later, Alicia headed to her coven meeting with more questions than answers. As she entered the meeting room, several of her coven sisters said hello.

"Welcome sister," they said in unison.

"Hi, sisters," Alicia replied.

At that precise moment, Laura stood and told everyone the meeting would be starting soon. Each and everyone in the room took their seats and waited patiently. Finally, Laura spoke.

"Good evening my coven sisters and brothers," she smiled as she looked around the room.

Everyone replied their hellos.

"We have lots to discuss today, but before we begin, I want to welcome a new member into our fold. Please give a warm welcome to our newest member, Valentino Perez," she said as she clapped.

Just as Laura said his name, he entered the room.

Alicia sat there without saying a word. She couldn't believe that Valentino was in the meeting, let alone that he was a warlock. How could she have missed that?

"Thank you everyone for the warm welcome. I look forward to getting to know each and every one of you," he said as his gaze fell on Alicia.

Sitting down he could feel Alicia's stare and smiled.

Laura continued with the meeting and at one point she cleared her throat to make sure everyone was paying attention.

"I have an announcement I want to share with all of you. I've been thinking of moving away from Wisterious Bay," she said looking around the room.

All at once several people expressed their disbelief and said how awful it would be if she moved away. Alicia was thinking the same thing, but wondered why would Laura who seemed to be happy all of a sudden announce she may be leaving Wisterious Bay. Could it have anything to do with the argument she witnessed? Alicia wondered but kept her thoughts to herself.

Before she could contemplate any further, Laura's announcement, she told everyone to hold hands indicating the meeting was almost over. After repeating the protection spell and thanking everyone for coming she stood and awaited what she knew was coming.

Many of the coven members circled her obviously wanting to know what brought about her announcement. Alicia chose to leave instead and decided she'd approach Laura another day.

Walking home she looked around at all the decorations. Every single storefront had some theme or another all different, but all similar in that they were obviously geared towards Halloween. She was glad Wisterious Bay held true to their traditions all year long. It allowed for Alicia to enjoy every aspect of being a witch in a witchy town.

By the time she got home, her familiars were in the living room along with Zoraida. She smiled at seeing them all getting along so well.

"Alicia, welcome home," Augustus announced.

"I see you guys are doing well," she smiled.

"Si, we've been having a great time," he replied.

"All of you?" she inquired looking at Zoraida.

She purred.

Alright, now I really need to find out if she can understand me, Alicia thought to herself.

"Zoraida, you must think I'm crazy, but can you understand me?" Alicia asked as Felix clapped his hands.

Purrrrr, was her response.

"Oh boy!" she claimed as she looked at Felix and Augustus. They nodded.

"Well, guys this is definitely going to be very interesting," she said as they all looked at her and she raised up her hands in defeat.

Alicia spent the rest of the evening talking to all three and asking their opinion on who could've killed Sam and their thoughts on the whole situation. By the time she was ready to go to bed, she'd made up her mind that soon she'd be able to start seeing a clearer picture.

The next morning, Alicia woke up and proceeded to feed Zoraida. She then showered, drank her morning coffee, dressed and said a silent protection spell as she closed the door to her home. She walked purposely that morning into town. As she waved hello to the regular early morning joggers she thought about Valentino.

Suddenly stopping in her tracks, she shook her head. She needed to stop obsessing over that man, especially now that she knew he was a warlock. How could she have been so blinded by his charisma that she missed the fact that he had magic in his blood. She wondered if he had placed some kind of spell on her to prevent her from seeing the real him. For that matter, she wondered if he also knew Sam from the time that he had dated Gertrude.

What worried Alicia was how she was going to find out anything about him if she couldn't be close enough to him without blushing or stumbling her words. Maybe she herself should do a spell to make her resilient to his charm, she pondered. But immediately dismissed it knowing it was not the way she wanted to handle the situation.

Arriving at the local hair salon she took a deep breath and put aside any more thoughts of Valentino, at least for awhile. As she entered, she realized the place was full. She never knew so many people frequented the salon so early in the morning.

"Good morning, Alicia, how have you been? Haven't seen you around here in a while," Catalina, the owner asked as she stood behind the counter.

"Good morning, Catalina. I'm so sorry. What with getting ready for the festivities and working on my new collection, you can imagine. And now with Sam's death, I haven't had time to breath let alone stop by, but here I am," she replied smiling as she looked around the salon.

Alicia noticed neither Meredith nor Dolores was there yet. That gave her plenty of time to be seated and not appear as if she was following Dolores.

"Sam," she said the words out loud with disgust.

"Did you not like Sam?" Alicia noticed how she said his name.

"Not in the least. He treated Dolores with no respect and besides I knew him from back when he lived here and he just wasn't a nice person," she replied.

"What was he like back then?" Alicia asked.

"Oh, I don't want to talk about him. Let's see who's going to work on you today," she said looking down at the appointment book and instantly changing the subject.

"Here you go, they're ready for you," and with that the conversation was over.

"Thank you," Alicia replied.

As Alicia walked to the empty chair, she wondered what Catalina knew about Sam that made her feel so strongly about him. As she pondered the idea, her thoughts were interrupted. She was told she needed to decide what she wanted done today, and so all thoughts of Catalina were put on hold.

Finally, she decided on highlights, a haircut, a pedicure and a manicure, basically the works. By the time Dolores entered the salon, Alicia had foils in her hair and looked like a very insane witch. She laughed before making eye contact with Dolores.

"What are you doing here?" Dolores demanded as she approached Alicia.

"Good morning, Dolores. Again, I'm so sorry for your loss, but you must know that I had nothing to do with Sam's death," she stressed the point.

Taking a deep breath, she nodded.

"I know, but I have no one else to blame. Besides, he never would've been there if it wasn't for you. I told him over and over again, but he didn't listen to me. Now look what that got him," she said as she turned around and walked to her chair before Alicia could ask what she meant.

Now why would she say it was my fault that got him killed, she thought to herself. This was getting very strange. Meredith interrupted her thoughts.

"Oye, prima. Penny for your thoughts," Meredith said.

"Sorry. I just had the strangest conversation with Dolores. Well not really a conversation as it was more one sided, but still. She said something very strange. She said Sam's death was my fault. She mentioned she had warned him repeatedly and he hadn't listened and look what that got him. Do you know anything about what she could've been talking about?" Alicia asked.

Meredith was about to answer when Sheriff McDonald walked into the salon straight to where they were standing.

"Good morning, ladies. Meredith, I need you to come to the station as soon as you're done here. I need to ask you some questions about Sam," he stated.

"Why would you need to ask her anything about Sam?" Alicia couldn't help herself.

"First of all, this does not concern you. Secondly, and I guess knowing this town the way I know it, everyone will know about it anyway soon enough so I'll tell you. But mind you, I expect you'll stay out of the investigation. I still have my doubts about you and your involvement in this case. So, no funny business. Anyway, the reason I want to speak with your cousin is that she was seen arguing with Sam shortly before he was killed," he stated rather exasperated with the whole situation.

"Wait what?" Alicia responded looking directly at Meredith.

Meredith on the other hand just looked down at her feet and avoided looking at Alicia.

"Did you hear what I said Meredith?" Sheriff McDonald stood stoic waiting for a response.

"Yes. I'll stop by the station as soon as I'm done here," she replied.

"Good. Well, if you'll both excuse me, I have lots to do," he said and left the salon without saying another word.

"Prima, want to explain what that was all about?" Alicia asked.

"No," Meredith responded and then walked over to an empty chair to await her turn.

Now Alicia was more confused than ever. First, Dolores was acting and saying things that didn't make any sense. And now, Meredith was the one avoiding talking about Sam. Alicia couldn't imagine why Meredith would've had words with Sam or what could've compelled them to argue? *Could she have been the person she saw arguing with Laura,* she thought to herself.

The size of the person arguing with Laura didn't fit Meredith's description. The person was somewhat taller and a bit heavier. Still, it was interesting that there was starting to be people in town that had a strong opinion about Sam.

For someone who wasn't that active in the community, he sure had made a significant number of waves in the time he had arrived in town. Between possible old wounds to new enemies, Sam had become one popular resident of Wisterious Bay.

Then it hit her like a ton of bricks. Meredith would need to be added to the suspect list.

As much as she hated thinking about it, Meredith was hiding something and the fact that she was seen arguing with him before he died unfortunately put her on top of her list.

By the time that Alicia was ready to leave, Dolores had departed without saying another word. Meredith did say goodbye, but briefly. She excused herself saying she needed to go see Sheriff McDonald and didn't want to make him wait any longer. Refusing to discuss Sam, she told Alicia she'd see her later.

When it was her turned to pay for the services, Alicia addressed Catalina.

"Thank you again for taking care of me in this morning. This was exactly what I needed," she smiled.

As she was presented with the bill, she made sure to include a tip for everyone that had worked on her that morning.

"By the way, I'd love to get a coffee and catch up. Are you available tomorrow morning?" she asked.

Catalina had no idea Alicia's sole purpose was to find out the story behind why she disliked Sam so much and to find out if she possibly could've been the killer.

Agreeing to meet for breakfast, Alicia suggested meeting the next morning at The Cauldron Coffee House. The time was set for eight o'clock. Saying goodbye to everyone Alicia exited the beauty salon.

As she stepped outside and looked around Alicia was debating whether to head to Patchouli Mystical Tesoros or the station. The fact that Meredith was avoiding her was an indication that she should drop the subject for now. However, that was difficult for Alicia and she decided instead to follow her instinct.

Closing her eyes, Alicia tried to think of anything except her prima. She refused to imagine that she had anything to do with Sam's death. Although, things were not looking good for her, she just couldn't fathom her prima killing anyone, let alone Sam.

So, she turned in the opposite direction of her shop and headed towards the station. As she walked Main Street, she purposely let her mind wander.

What she didn't anticipate was where her thoughts ended. Of all people, Valentino. She couldn't help but remember his physique, followed by his muscles and that wicked smile. That first time she saw him at the bakery dressed in that suit... the vision was forever sealed in her mind.

Chapter 8

Now Alicia had formulated a credible list of potential suspects. The names let her establish a priority system with specific details for each individual she intended to interview.

Sadly, she looked at the list again reading over Meredith's name out loud. Hoping against all hope Meredith would be removed from the list soon. She decided one way to expedite the matter was to approach Gertrude first, as she would be most accessible.

Heading over to Patchouli Mystical Tesoros, Alicia thought about how to start the conversation so it didn't seem as if she was accusing her of anything in particular. In record time she reached the shop and pushed open the door. Gertrude was standing behind the counter rearranging a display of sample size candles.

"Good morning, Gertrude," Alicia said as she closed the door behind her.

"Good morning. How was your evening?" She asked.

"Well, you may not know but I finally have a familiar. Haydee's cat had kittens and I decided to take one of them and I'm so excited. I've already named her. I'm calling her Zoraida," Alicia beamed.

"What a wonderful name. Zoraida," Gertrude repeated the name out loud smiling.

"She's a welcomed addition to the family," Alicia replied as she headed back to her office.

Dropping off her jacket and purse, she went into the kitchen. She noticed Gertrude had already started the coffee and had also set the pastries on a round plate. Walking back out she took a deep breath and looked directly at Gertrude.

"Thank you for making the coffee this morning. Before we turn over the Open sign, I wanted to address something with you," she stated.

"Sure, what's up?" Gertrude asked not realizing Alicia would be asking about Sam.

She started purposely slow as to not come on too strong.

"I'm certain you're aware that Sam was found right here in the shop," she said pointing to the center of the room.

Gertrude remained quiet.

"And, you may have heard by now that Sheriff McDonald is speaking to Meredith. According to a witness someone saw her and Sam arguing before he died," Alicia said and waited to see if Gertrude would say something.

Since she remained quiet, Alicia continued.

"I'm trying to find out as much as possible about Sam in hopes of finding the killer before McDonald decides Meredith is the killer or worse me, for having been the one to find him," she stated.

"Sheriff McDonald I'm sure, realizes neither of you could've killed Sam. He's just doing his job in trying to eliminate suspects, that's all," she responded.

"Well, for that reason and to make sure he does just that, I need to ask you to tell me what you know about Sam. I know you dated him in the past and it's obvious it must have ended badly. But please consider helping me out and telling what you know, it's important," Alicia said as she placed her hand over Gertrude's hand and squeezed.

Taking a deep breath and closing her eyes Gertrude contemplated whether she should tell her about her time with Sam. It had been so long ago, she wanted to forget and yet here she was again having to think about it. Finally opening her eyes, she looked directly at Alicia.

"There's really nothing to tell. He lived here a long time ago. We dated briefly, he moved away, it ended, and that was that. Next time I saw him is when he moved back into town with Dolores. I tried to avoid him as much as possible. It didn't seem he'd changed much and I didn't want to be reminded of what an unpleasant man he was, so I avoided him. There's nothing else to say," she replied removing her hand from the counter.

"Now, if you'll excuse me, I want to check on our inventory," Gertrude said and walked away leaving Alicia pondering what she'd just said.

It wasn't much and unfortunately knowing somewhat of the reason why she didn't like him was not helping her. So, for now, she remained on the list. Before she knew it the shop was filled with customers and the rest of the day went by fairly quickly. By the time they were ready to close neither had mentioned Sam again.

"I'll close up," Alicia informed Gertrude.

"Are you sure?" she asked.

"Yes, it's been a long day and I can definitely stay. Why don't you go home and have an early evening," she encouraged Gertrude.

"Sure, thanks," she replied smiling.

Alicia walked around the shop blowing out the candles and noticed Gertrude hesitate at the door.

"Is everything alright?" She asked.

"Yes, it just occurred to me that I'm making dinner for myself and Valentino. Why don't you join us tonight?" She asked.

"Dinner with you and Valentino?" She cautiously asked.

Alicia wasn't sure she'd be able to behave normally in front of Valentino. But then again, this would give her an opportunity to question him about Sam. Even if that meant Gertrude would get mad at her.

"Sure, I'd love to join you both for dinner. What time and what can I bring?" Alicia asked.

"Nothing, I have everything covered. See you tonight at eight o'clock. Oh, and by the way, I love your new look," Gertrude said as she left the shop.

After she had walked out Alicia wondered if she'd made a mistake by accepting the dinner invitation. She wondered if Gertrude was doing this to find out how much information Alicia had gathered or if it was indeed just an innocent invitation.

She finished cleaning up and ensuring the back door and front door were both locked before making a stop in her lab. She wanted to see if she could find something in the spell book that would expedite the truth coming out. Maybe she could actually create a specific candle that in the presence of Valentino would at least work on him if not on Gertrude.

However, she needed to be careful. Him being a warlock, he might be aware it was a magical candle. She decided to make a small batch an existing candle and used her spell which brought clarity. Hopefully, someone would open up to speak their mind, whether it was the truth or not. Maybe this was all she needed.

Once she had finished, she gathered her sample, grabbed a basket and a bottle of wine she had in the cooler and wrapped it all in a bright orange ribbon. It was the perfect gift to bring to dinner. Gertrude would think it was one of the *normal* candles and not think anything of it being possibly magical.

Alicia locked up her lab and closed the wall. She then turned off all the lights and locked the shop. Heading home, she was careful with the package. She didn't want it to fall. When she arrived home, she placed it in the entryway ready to take when she headed out to dinner.

Knowing Zoraida was probably hungry, she called out her name as she walked towards the kitchen. There the kitten waited by her bowl.

"Boy you really are something," Alicia chuckled as she grabbed some food.

Zoraida purred and circled Alicia's leg as she poured out her dinner.

Opening the can of cat food, she told Zoraida about her day and asked if she'd be willing to follow her to Gertrude's house. And if so, would she be willing to stay in the background, hidden. All she needed her to do was observe. She was certain Valentino or maybe even Gertrude would reveal something that evening that would move them up on the suspect list.

"Well, if you decide to follow me tonight, just remember, it's pertinent that you stay out of sight. Valentino being a warlock will know you belong to me. And, once Felix and Augustus wake up, tell them I need them too. If this is going to be a joint effort, I'm going to need all the help I can get," she said as she looked at Zoraida.

Zoraida meowed instead of speaking as she was too busy cleaning herself.

Alicia understood her response and was grateful to know she'd be there in case anything happened. Shortly after having tried more than twenty outfits, Alicia settled on a flannel skirt with a cotton long sleeve shirt and boots. All earth tones which complimented her skin color, hair and eyes.

Nervous she headed for the door, grabbed the basket and exited walking towards Gertrude's house. She stopped short of approaching the front door and thought she'd made a mistake. She was about to turn around and leave thinking of the excuse she'd say to Gertrude when she ran right into Valentino.

"You know, we really do need to stop meeting this way," Valentino said as he smiled devilishly at Alicia.

"Why do you keep doing that?" Alicia asked trying not to sound frustrated.

"Me? You're the one that bumped into me. I was minding my own business heading to the front door when you turned around abruptly and ran right into my arms," now he was chuckling.

"You think this is funny?" she looked ashen.

"Yes," he continued to laugh making Alicia also laugh.

Next thing they knew they were both laughing so hard Gertrude opened the door to find out what the commotion was all about.

"Well, I see you two are hitting it off," she smiled as she stood at her door.

They both looked at each other and at the same time said.

"Truce?"

Agreeing they both climbed the stairs and followed Gertrude inside.

Alicia walked in ahead of Valentino and placed the basket on the foyer table. Picking up the bottle she handed it to Gertrude.

"I know you told me not to bring anything, but you know me I couldn't come to dinner and not bring something," she smiled.

Gertrude thanked her and took the bottle to the bar area to open.

Alicia then removed the candle from the basket and placed it on the fireplace mantle. And lit it before she turned around.

"I know this is your favorite," Alicia said as she turned around and lit the candle.

If anyone noticed she had brought her own matches, no one said anything.

She'd also been practicing a fairly simple spell of meditation for visualizing calm boundaries. Figuring she needed it now more than ever; she sat on the couch while Gertrude was busy in the kitchen and Valentino was somewhere else in the house.

Normally, this spell was done in the kitchen with a candle, candleholder, water, and a sachet of herbal tea. But lately she'd been finding a way to still do the spell when needed without the physical items.

Having adjusted one of the spells from her mother's spell book, she instead visualized the items each doing what they were intended to do.

She visualized the water as her emotions. Breathing deeply, she pictured herself floating in the water and relaxing. This made her feel secure, confident, and safe inside Gertrude's home. She also imagined her familiars, including Zoraida protecting her.

Once she felt it was time, she imagined pouring the water into a kettle and bringing it to boil. Once the water boiled, she poured herself an imaginary cup of tea.

Looking around to make sure no one was near, she picked up the imaginary cup of tea and drank. She then blew her breath out as if she had extinguished the candle and then placing the tea cup on the table took one last breath in and out.

At that point Valentino entered where Alicia was sitting. He could feel the shift in the air as did she. Looking up Alicia smiled. Valentino returned the smile.

"So, I heard you're moving into the Henderson Home," Alicia said as she looked into his eyes.

She could feel the flutter of butterflies, but was able to abate them and continue without lumbering her words.

"Yes. I actually move into the house tomorrow. I'm looking forward to spending time here in Wisterious Bay," he replied.

"This is a great place to live. I can't imagine living anywhere else," she said as she thought about what her life had been like before moving into town, and most importantly that she was in the same room as Valentino and not blushing or stammering her words.

"Ahem, I was wondering if I could ask you a question?" Alicia said as she looked into his eyes.

Smiling, he nodded.

"Can you tell me anything at all about Gertrude's breakup with Sam?" She asked looking back in the direction of the kitchen to make sure Gertrude's was out of site.

"Sure, back in the day, especially for a while everything was great. They spent all their time together. That is until the day she tried to kill him."

Chapter 9

"Stop right there! I did not try to kill Sam," Gertrude growled as she placed her hands on her hip.

Alicia wondered where Gertrude had come from as she was certain when she looked back, she had not been standing anywhere nearby.

Looking directly at Alicia. Gertrude made it perfectly clear the walls in her house were paper thin.

"Fine. You didn't try to kill him. Can we move on please?" Valentino huffed and walked to the other side of the room to serve himself a drink. He knew what happened that day long ago, but it wasn't his place to tell the story, so he remained silent.

Taking a deep breath Gertrude tried to explain.

"Look we were in love, or at least that's what I thought. The idea was that we were going to buy a house, get married, and have children, blah blah blah," she paused before continuing.

"I thought everything was going great until one day, a week before the wedding, he came to me and said he was leaving town. He'd changed his mind and needed to explore the world," again, she paused, this time closing her eyes.

Alicia was afraid to say anything that would stop Gertrude from speaking so she remained quiet as did Valentino.

"The thought of losing him and then it being so close to the wedding made me crazy. I ran outside and got behind the wheel of my car. Just as I was pulling out, he jumped in front as if he could magically stop the car. At that same moment Valentino pulled up. He came up to my window and with his stretched arm turned off the engine," she said as she looked at Alicia defeated and obviously shaken from rehashing the past.

"I'm sorry to have made you bring up that memory. I never meant to... I'm sorry," Alicia didn't finish the sentence.

"It's fine. I would never have deliberately run him over. It's just that... mi prima here likes to tease me about it and say he saved Sam that day, when in reality like I stressed to him over and over again, I never would have pressed the peddle," Gertrude answered taking another deep breath.

"Look the only reason I still feel bitter is because when he finally returned home, he acted as if nothing had ever happened between us. He flaunted Dolores like she was the best thing that ever happened to him, and I guess I was a bit jealous. But I did *not* kill Sam," she stated with conviction.

"Again, I'm really sorry for prying. It's just that I need to find out what happened to Sam and I thought maybe you could shed some light into his past," Alicia said without mentioning she had considered Gertrude a suspect.

"But wait you did try to kill him with your car!" Valentino laughed trying to breaking the ice.

"Funny," Gertrude replied and at this point also started laughing.

Soon all three were laughing so hard the negative feeling that had hung in the air dissipated.

"So, when are we eating?" Valentino asked obviously hungry and ready to change the subject.

"That's what I was coming out to tell you both. Dinner will be ready in five," she replied and waving her hand retreated back into the kitchen.

By the time dessert was served, they had all forgotten about Sam. They talked about Wisterious Bay and growing up in town and how Gertrude never wanted to leave compared to Valentino. He assured them he was happy to return and was even thinking of moving back permanently.

During this time, he snuck peeks at Alicia watching her reaction. She smiled internally not giving too much away, but it was obvious the news pleased her.

Gertrude finally noticed something brewing between Alicia and Valentino, and she liked the possibility of that happening. She loved them both and the thought of them getting together made her very happy.

At the same time, Alicia asked Valentino something that had been brewing in her mind since she saw him at the coven meeting.

"So, how do you know Laura?" She looked at him and noticed immediately something that told her not to pursue that line of questioning.

"Laura? You know Laura?" Gertrude asked.

"I just met her the other day when I was walking around Main Street and walked into her shop.

"What could you possibly be doing inside Lotions & Things? Since when do you use lotion?" Gertrude asked.

Valentino looked at Alicia when he answered.

"I was curious about what she sold and wanted to introduced myself as the newbie in town," he answered.

That's when it dawned on her that Gertrude didn't know he was a warlock or at least that he was familiar with magic.

Interesting, she thought. She'd have to inquire more about that, but for now she got the hint and said nothing.

By the time Alicia left, she was feeling better about Gertrude's connection to Sam. She decided to still keep an eye out, but in her mind moved her to the bottom of the list.

As she entered her house, her familiars and Zoraida were all hanging out by the fireplace waiting for her arrival.

If this was to become a regular occurrence Alicia decided she liked the site of all three hanging out together.

"So, I take it everything went well after we left?" Felix asked.

"Yes, as a matter-of-fact Gertrude opened up about her relationship with Sam. I don't think she's the killer, but I'm not crossing her off the list completely. The thing is I do feel safe around her, so I'm certain there's nothing to worry about. It's obvious she still held a grudge and was badly hurt, but maybe now she can finally move on and hopefully forget all about Sam and what he did to her all those years ago," she sighed.

"We've discussed it and don't feel she's the killer either," Augustus replied.

"Well, then first thing tomorrow morning I'm meeting with Catalina from the hair salon. I'll see if I can get anything out of her. She's the next one on the list," Alicia said as she went to the fireplace to light the fire.

Once the fire was going strong, Alicia grabbed a book and sat down in her favorite chair. She then picked up Zoraida and placed her on her lap. She purred as she adjusted herself and closed her eyes. Alicia enjoyed reading a few chapters every night before heading to bed.

Smiling she stroked Zoraida while Felix and Augustus attempted to play a game of chess. A site no one would believe unless they saw it firsthand.

The next morning Alicia headed out to The Cauldron Coffee House to meet up with Catalina as they had arranged. She had arranged to meet Catalina about an hour before Laura and Meredith were expected to arrive for their daily morning get together.

Looking around the coffee house she headed towards the corner table in the back. She figured if Catalina was going to talk, moving away from piercing eyes and nosy townspeople would help.

"Good morning, Alicia. You're here early today?" She was asked.

"Buenos dias. Si, I'm actually meeting Catalina. You know Catalina from the hair salon?" Alicia asked.

"Oh yes, she comes here often for breakfast. I'll bring you your coffee and once she's here I'll take your orders," she replied as she walked away.

Shortly after that Catalina walked into the coffee house and seeing Alicia in the corner waved. As she approached the table she yawned.

"Good morning. Sorry I didn't sleep well last night and had a hard time getting up," Catalina yawned again.

"I'm sorry. Why didn't you just cancel?" Alicia asked.

"That's alright. I needed to get up anyway. Have lots to do this morning before I open up the salon. I don't know where everyone is coming from, but it seems I'm fully booked for the next two weeks. It's crazy how this time of year gets in Wisterious Bay," she said as she sat down.

Shortly after the waitress returned, she placed a cup of coffee in front of Alicia, and waited to take everyone's order. Once they had decided what we wanted to eat Alicia turned on her sleuthing hat.

"So, how do you like living in Wisterious Bay?" Alicia asked.

"I've lived here for so long it's second nature. I really can't see myself living anywhere else," she said with a smile.

"I have to agree with you. Once I arrived in town everyone was so welcoming including you, it's been wonderful. I too can't see myself living anywhere else. That's why I'm so concerned about Sam and who could've killed him. It's stressing me out, especially that there may be a killer lose in our town. Also, I don't want Sheriff McDonald to blame the murder on me. I don't know why, but I think he has it out for me," she stated chuckling.

Alicia knew exactly why Sheriff McDonald behaved the way he did, she just chose to ignore him when possible. She did wonder sometimes if he'd ever get past the fact that she solved those murders before he did. Or if he would hold that against her for the rest of her life, hopefully not.

"Why would he blame the murder on you? There's lots of people who didn't like Sam," she stated matter of fact.

This was exactly what Alicia had hoped would happen. The perfect segway.

"So, then you must've known Sam well, at least back when he used to live here?" Alicia asked.

Obviously, Catalina didn't want to respond as she looked away with a faraway look. It took her a few minutes to finally speak.

"Look I don't necessarily want to talk about Sam. Suffice to say he was not an honest person. And although I don't particularly like Dolores, I can't help but feel bad for her. Again, I'm not saying anything, but maybe she finally had enough of Sam," she replied bitterly.

Interesting how she deflected talking too much about her past especially that it looks like they may have at some point had something going on between them, Alicia thought to herself.

Alicia wondered how many people had crossed Sam.

"Maybe you should consider speaking with Dolores?" Catalina suggested.

"I have tried, but she seems to think I had something to do with his murder," Alicia replied.

"Not surprised she hasn't accused more people," Catalina stated.

Alicia waited to see if she'd elaborate and when Catalina remained quiet, she asked what she meant.

"What do you mean?" Alicia inquired.

"As I already mentioned, Sam was not an honest person. Now, let's leave it at that and change the subject please," she said and took a bite of her breakfast.

"So, are you doing anything special for the festivities this year?" Alicia asked.

"I'm so busy with this month's appointments I won't have time for anything else. Although I've been meaning on stopping by your shop to buy some candles for the salon," Catalina replied.

"Wonderful. Come by anytime. I'll even give you the family and friends discount," she said as she smiled warmly.

The rest of the breakfast was spent talking about the number of tourists that had descended onto Wisterious Bay and how they couldn't wait until everything returned to normal.

As Catalina left The Cauldron Coffee House, she informed Alicia she'd stop by the shop later that afternoon.

Alicia sat back down to wait for Laura and Meredith. She thought about everything or mostly what little information Catalina had provided. One thing was certain, she needed to speak with Dolores whether she wanted to or not.

The bell on the door rang as it was opened. Alicia smiled and waved at Meredith.

"Buenos dias prima. How's it going?" Meredith smiled as she sat down.

"Bien. Aquí," Alicia replied.

"Did I just see Catalina leaving the coffee house?" Meredith inquired.

"Yes, we had an early breakfast. I wanted to catch up with her and figured her coming here made it easier to stay and meet up with you and Laura after she left," Alicia replied.

"Catch up? Or are you sleuthing again?" Meredith asked arching her eyebrows.

"Yeah, yeah. You know me too well. Look, I need to figure out who killed Sam! If I leave it up to Sherriff McDonald, he may arrest me for the crime. So, I'm going to do what I need to do, to get to the bottom of this case," Alicia tried to sound serious.

"I know you well enough. Esta bien. If you need help, let me know," Meredith stated hoping Alicia would not ask her to help.

"No te preocupes. I've got it under control," Alicia replied.

Meredith thanked the heavens mentally. She didn't really want anything to do with Sam or who killed him. Only, if Alicia was in trouble would she freely help.

"By the way, Laura is late? Have you spoken with her lately?" Alicia asked.

"No. As a matter of fact. She's been acting rather distant lately," Meredith replied.

"Well, after announcing she's planning on moving, I realized something was off with her. I hope it's not anything serious. She's been having some health issues lately, but I thought they were minor," Alicia responded.

"Yeah. Bueno, I'll go see Laura later," Meredith smiled as the food was placed on the table.

Just then the waitress placed their plates on the table.

"Your usual ladies, enjoy."

For the next hour they talked about everything except Sam. It was refreshing spending time again with Meredith without having to think about a victim.

When they were done, they walked out together. The weather was brisk so each of them zipped up their jackets. Meredith then headed to Hannah's Tea House and Alicia towards her Patchouli Mystical Tesoros Shop.

As Alicia entered the shop, Gertrude was busy lighting candles and setting out the coffee and pastries for the customers.

"Buenos dias, Gertrude," Alicia said as she smiled.

"Buenos dias," Gertrude replied.

"That's great. You'll be speaking Spanish soon," Alicia smiled.

"I hope so!" Gertrude replied.

Right before turning over the sign from closed to open Alicia told Gertrude, she'd be heading out soon to run errands. She didn't feel the need to tell her that she was planning on stopping by at the station and to see Dolores.

Walking out with two bags of an assortment of candles from the shop she told Gertrude she'd be available on her cell if she needed her.

Next stop was the station to see if she could find out where they were with the investigation.

"Who are you again?" the officer asked as she looked at Alicia over her spectacles.

Alicia noticed this was a new addition to the Sheriff's office. She handed her the bag with goodies and said it was compliments of Patchouli Mystical Tesoros Shop. The officer, a woman appeared to be in her early sixties. She had grayish hair and dark brown eyes. As she sat behind the counter, she glanced into the bag then set it aside without uttering even a word.

"I'm Alicia, Sam's body was found in my shop," she answered.

The deputy scowled.

"Well, I can't speak to you about an ongoing investigation. Now if you'll excuse me, I'm very busy," The officer said.

"Can I see Sheriff McDonald?" she asked without thinking.

Looking up from her spectacles the officer chuckled before responding.

"Your funeral," she said as she stood and walked to the back of the station.

Within minutes Sheriff McDonald came out and walked directly up to Alicia.

"What do you want? Can't you see I'm a busy man?" McDonald basically growled.

Swallowing, she tried to sound calm.

"I was wondering if there were any new developments on the case?" Alicia asked him.

"Sure, do you want to hear about them?" he asked.

"Why yes," she couldn't believe he would actually tell her and just as quickly her hopes dwindled.

Laughing he nodded his head side to side as he rolled his eyes.

"No, I'm not going to discuss with you an open case. Now leave and let me get back to work," he said still laughing as he walked away.

Well, that went well, she thought to herself as she exited the station.

There's no way she was giving up on the investigation. Just because she couldn't get anything out of McDonald didn't mean she didn't have other means of finding out information.

Dolores was sitting out on her porch rocking with her eyes closed when Alicia approached.

"Good day, Dolores," Alicia smiled.

Opening her eyes, she squinted and brought her eyebrows together. "You!" That's all she said.

"I bring a peace offering," Alicia said as she climbed the stairs and handed Dolores the bag with goodies.

Dolores inspected the bag and sighed.

"You might as well sit," she indicated to Alicia to come sit in the empty chair next to her on the porch.

"Gracias," Alicia replied.

Dolores looked in the bag and took out the candles smelling them one by one.

"These are amazing!" she said cheerfully.

"My pleasure. I figured you could use something nice. I know you are still mourning, but this might cheer you up a little bit," Alicia replied.

"So, I'm sure you stopped by for another reason. Let's have it," Dolores looked directly at Alicia.

Swallowing she spoke.

"Well, as I mentioned already, I'm hoping you can shed some light as to who could've wanted Sam dead?" Alicia asked.

Laughing a hearty laugh, she replied.

"Oh Alicia, you're so clueless. My darling, everyone wanted Sam dead, including me," Dolores laughed diabolically.

Chapter 10

"Wait what?" Alicia asked.

"You should know by now that Sam was not a very likable person. In fact, everywhere he went, he left behind broken hearts and disgruntled ... let's just say a lot of people didn't like Sam," Dolores stated.

"I didn't realize so many people disliked him," Alicia replied.

"Well, there you go. Now you know," Dolores shrugged her shoulders.

"How long had you known Sam?" Alicia asked.

"Long enough. In the end I just got sick and tired of worrying if he was with someone else or what his motivation was behind whatever he was doing. I'd just had enough. So, he'll not be missed. At least not by me," Dolores made a face that was obvious to anyone that she couldn't care less about Sam. Her eyebrows were lowered forming a 'V' above the nose which produced wrinkles on her forehead.

Thinking more and more that Dolores was the killer, Alicia realized she needed to make Dolores confess to the murder. *But how to do that*, she thought to herself.

"I'm sorry it had to end the way it did. Didn't you ever think about just leaving instead?" Alicia prompted.

Laughing Dolores shook her head. She had such a crazed look that Alicia didn't know how to respond. Then all of a sudden, she started to laugh again, this time hysterically. She even rolled over and held her stomach as she continued to laugh.

"Did I say something funny?" Alicia asked concerned Dolores was starting to lose it.

"Yes. Indeed, you did. Leaving him... as if that was an option. Besides, this time he had a crazy idea that was starting to look promising. But of course, he messed it up as usual. Now, I have to figure out how to get out of dodge, and soon," she stated abruptly standing up.

Startled Alicia she didn't know how to respond. Following Dolores, she too stood thinking this visit is over.

"Alrighty, now. It's time for you to leave," Dolores demanded as she placed her hands on her hips.

"Aw, oh of course. Sorry to have taken up your time. I hope you enjoy your gift, and I guess I'll see you around town," Alicia said as she turned around and walked down the stairs.

"Don't count on it," Dolores called out and she walked inside and slammed the door.

Alicia couldn't wait until she got home to talk to her Felix, Augustus, and of course Zoraida. She needed to run by them everything that had happened from talking to Catalina, to Meredith, and now Dolores even if it wasn't much information.

It was becoming more and more obvious that Dolores was the killer and she needed their help to figure out a way to get her to confess. From all accounts, she was jealous of anyone who spoke to Sam. No one could blame her for that as he was the town flirt. He even had a history with several of the women in town, Gertrude and Catalina were two she knew about for certain.

Alicia couldn't use the excuse of stopping by again with another gift. That would definitely not fly. And if she was going to do anything about it, it had to be soon as Dolores appeared to be planning on leaving town any day. That in itself was a lucky break as Zoraida had apparently

Her mind was reeling as she approached Patchouli Mystical Tesoros. She'd been gone long enough and she needed to check in on Gertrude and see how everything was going on in the shop.

As she was walking on Main Street, she saw Sheriff McDonald. She was tempted to stop him and tell him her suspicions about Dolores. However, she knew he'd just blow her off and warn her again not to get involved in police business.

The only way to convince him that she's the killer was to show him the proof. An idea was brewing in her mind and she needed her peeps to help her come up with a plan. If everything worked out according to her calculations, they would get Dolores to confess before she had a chance to leave Wisterious Bay.

"You're back," Gertrude said as Alicia walked in the door.

At this point the shop was full of customers. Alicia apologized for being late and got to work. Several hours later they were able to take a break. They headed back to the kitchen area and sat for a few minutes.

"I can't believe it's been nonstop," Gertrude stated.

"Where is everyone coming from? They're not really supposed to be here until next week?" Alicia stated without really expecting an answer.

"Right? It's insane. I guess there's been enough advertising that people have descended on our town earlier than expected," Gertrude replied.

"At least we're stocked up and we have plenty of inventory. Although if you notice we need to replenish anything in particular, let me know," Alicia stated.

"Will do. By the way, did you hear that Dolores is putting up her house for sale?" Gertrude asked.

"No, but somehow, I knew it. My gut kept telling me that she'd be skipping town soon. How'd you find out?" Alicia was not very curious to hear her response.

"My neighbor is a realtor in town and asked me if I knew of anyone interested in purchasing Dolores's house as it was going to be placed on the market in the next few days," she replied.

Before Alicia could pursue the conversation any further, the doorbell jingled. They got up from the kitchen table and both walked out. Alicia stopped abruptly when she realized the customer was none other than Valentino.

Gertrude ran into Alicia knocking her across the room into his arms.

"Oh no! I'm so sorry Alicia. Are you alright? I was running to help you and didn't realize you had stopped," Gertrude said concerned.

At this point Alicia was trying to gather any dignity she had left before looking up at Valentino and hoping against all odds he didn't make a sly remark.

"So, I see you can't keep your hands off of me," Valentino chuckled.

Nope, too late.

"Ugh. Do you always have to be so... so..." she didn't finish the words. She had nothing to say. Anything she would say he'd use it against her and continue to make fun.

"Hey, leave her alone. This is my fault," Gertrude went up to Valentino and punched him in the arm.

"Ouch," he replied trying to hold back a grin.

"Very funny," Gertrude said.

"What do you want?" Alicia realized the moment she said it how it sounded.

"Sorry, I didn't mean to snap at you. It's just that you make me feel..." she stopped midway.

"I make you feel something? Now that, I like," he smiled this time tenderly.

That was Gertrude's cue to go back to the kitchen.

"Oh, I forgot something I needed to do in the back room. I'll be back," she said and walked away leaving them alone in the shop.

They stood there for a few seconds without saying anything to each other, and then he shuffled his feet until he looked directly into Alicia's eyes. Taking a deep breath as if trying to muster the courage to speak he stated the reason he had stopped by the shop.

"Actually, I came in here to ask you out to dinner," Valentino finally said.

"With me?" Alicia asked. She was so nervous she couldn't think of anything else to say.

"Well, you are the only person in here besides myself," now he chuckled.

"It's just that I haven't been on a date for so long. You caught me off guard," Alicia replied.

"Is that a good thing or a bad thing? It would be nice to get an answer," and now, he was starting to sound confident.

Smiling Alicia replied.

"Yes, I'd love to go out with you on a date," Alicia said as looked into his eyes.

"Perfect. I'll look at my calendar and get back to you," Valentino held back a grin.

"What?" Alicia was so taken aback that she didn't notice he was joking.

"Wait! No! I'm sorry. I was kidding. I guess I should have thought this one through. Again, I'm sorry," Valentino fumbled with his words.

This time he sounded sincere.

"You do have a unique sense of humor," Alicia replied smiling.

"Let's start over again. Hi, I'm here to see if you'd like to go to dinner with me tomorrow night?" Valentino asked.

"Why Valentino. This is so unexpected. I'll have to think about it," she now was laughing.

"Touché!" he too laughed.

"Yes, I'd love to go to dinner with you tomorrow night," Alicia blushed.

"Wonderful! It's a date. Can I have your number so I can text you the time?" Valentino asked.

"Sure," Alicia gave him her number and he added it to his cell.

"Before I go, I'd like to get a few candles," Valentino whispered.

"Oh, that kind. Sure, what are you looking for?" she too whispered.

"I've been feeling as if someone is watching me. It only happens at night. I don't feel threatened or anything. I just want to know their intentions," Valentino stated.

Alicia knew immediately who he was talking about. Wait until she got home and had a stern talking to her familiars. She repeatedly told them to stay out of sight and if they did venture outside the house, they needed to always make sure no one could spot them.

How on earth would she explain to people that she has a talking skeleton and a reaper of all things living in her house?

Not wanting to be obvious, she suggested a candle that although had magic didn't really reveal the intention of who he thought was watching him.

"How about my "Hit the Spot" candle? It's a combination of sage, rosemary, and lavender. It's very popular and usually we run out pretty early in the season," she asked him wondering if he would be interested.

Hit the Spot, was mostly for cleansing and protection. So, it was safe to offer it to him and she wouldn't have to worry about her familiar's being revealed to him, at least not yet.

"Sounds like that's exactly what I need. I'll take four candles," Valentino said as he took out his wallet.

"They're on the house. Sort of a welcoming and house warming gift," she smiled as she went to grab the candles.

Alicia wrapped them up in tissue paper and placed them inside a gift bag. Handing it over to him just as Gertrude returned.

"Oye Prima. What'd you buy?" she asked looking from Alicia to Valentino.

She wondered if anything had happened while she was away.

"Oh, just buying some candles for the house. As a matter of fact, I'm thinking of having a house warming get together. What do you think?" he asked them both.

"Sounds like fun. I can help with the decorations," Gertrude replied.

"And, I can invite a few of the locals?" Alicia asked.

"That's great guys. I really appreciate it. Now that I've decided to stay it's important to officially introduce myself in the community," Valentino replied.

"When were you thinking of having the party?" Alicia inquired.

"I still want to finish buying a few more items for the house. Even though I'm renting they've guaranteed it can be a long-term rental and I want the house to feel cozy. Once I've purchased a home I can then either take what I've bought or buy something new," he replied.

"Alright. Let us know when you're ready," Gertrude answered for both of them.

"Sounds like a plan. Thanks again for the candles," he said as he smiled at Alicia.

"My pleasure," she replied smiling.

"See you tomorrow night," Valentino said as he quickly exited the shop knowing if he didn't, he'd get the third degree from Gertrude.

"What is he talking about?" Gertrude asked Alicia.

Sighing she figured everyone in town was going to know soon enough anyway so she might as well tell her.

"Valentino asked me out to dinner for tomorrow night and I accepted," Alicia cringed knowing how she'd react.

Sure, enough Gertrude jumped up and down clapping her hands. Alicia laughed.

"This is wonderful! I knew there was something brewing between you two. I could tell from the way you both looked at each other that there was something there," she hugged Alicia tightly.

"It's just a dinner date," Alicia replied.

Ignoring her Gertrude clapped her hands again.

Rolling her eyes but smiling she walked away. Gertrude was so happy she could burst at the seams. She felt it in her bones, this was going to be good. Now, to figure out a way to make sure they stay together she smiled as she rubbed her hands together.

Gertrude decided to discuss the possibilities with Meredith. She'd definitely help make this work. She and her had been talking recently about Alicia's lack of a love life. Wait until she told her that her cousin, Valentino had actually asked Alicia out to dinner.

"Alicia, I need to step out for a moment," she said hoping Alicia wouldn't ask where she was going.

Well, there goes her wish.

"Where are you going?" Alicia asked suspiciously. She could feel Gertrude was planning something.

"Oh. Ah. Just over to get some more snacks for the shop. We're low and you know our customers love to stop by and take a nibble with their coffee or tea," she answered.

Looking over at the table, Alicia noticed it wouldn't hurt to get some more pastries.

"Fine. But you better not be sneaking off to plan anything," Alicia stated.

Gertrude ignored her and as she was walking out the door replied.

"Can't hear you," laughing she closed the door behind her.

Oh boy, by the end of the day everyone in town was going to know that she was going to dinner with Valentino, she thought to herself as she nodded her head side to side.

It was rather exciting to finally be going out on a date. It had been so long she couldn't remember the last time she felt this elated. And, to think that Valentino might feel the same was nerve wrecking.

Gertrude ran over to Hannah's Tea House. She pushed the door open and signaled to Meredith.

"Is everything alright?" Meredith asked startled at Gertrude's outburst.

Out of breath, she nodded. She was so happy she could hardly speak.

"Guess what?" Gertrude asked.

"What? The Pope is coming to town?" Meredith was clueless as to what would have her so gleeful.

"Very funny! No. Valentino just asked Alicia out to dinner and she said yes," Gertrude replied while doing a happy dance.

"Really? That's great news. Hey everyone, Alicia is going out to dinner with Valentino - Gertrude's cousin who just moved into town," Meredith called out to everyone that was in the tea house.

And there it began...

Chapter 11

By the time it was closing time Alicia was so tired she wasn't thinking any more about her date with Valentino. All she wanted to do was go home, take a hot bath, and sit by the fire with Felix, Augustus, and Zoraida.

"I'll close up tonight. Why don't you head out," Alicia told Gertrude.

"Are you sure? I don't mind closing shop tonight," she replied.

"No, that's alright. I've got it. You go on home. I'll only be a little while anyway," Alicia said to her as she shushed her towards the door.

"Thanks. See you tomorrow. Have a great evening," Gertrude said as she gathered her jacket and closed the door behind her.

Alicia followed, locked the door and turned over the sign to Closed. Walking around the shop she began to blow out the candles. She hadn't noticed how tired she was until she blew out the last candle and took a deep breath.

She'd decided to go down to her lab for a moment when she walked up to the wall and noticed it was not completely closed. She wondered if Gertrude had seen the wall protruding out and if so, why hadn't she said anything. Then she realized if she had, she definitely would have mentioned it. She probably was distracted and left it that way herself.

Shrugging her shoulders, she pulled open the wall and turned on the light as she descended the stairs. Suddenly, she smelled a scent that was familiar to her, but she couldn't place.

Looking around she wondered if someone had found her lab? And more importantly why would someone be interested in her lab? Cautiously she searched every inch of the lab. Nothing seemed to have been touched or disturbed.

Alicia doubted herself. Ignoring the prickling sensation on the back of her neck she checked on her herbs and made a mental note of those she needed to replenish. She'd grab some from her garden in the morning and bring some to the shop. It'd be easy to bring down to the lab when Gertrude went to lunch.

Not thinking any more about a possible intruder, she climbed back up the stairs and turned off the light. This time she made sure the wall was securely closed. What Alicia did not notice because she was so tired was that someone was watching her. There had been someone in her lab and that someone was the killer.

She did a final walk through to made sure the coffee pot and cups were put in the dishwasher, all of the candles had been blown out, and then she make sure the alleyway door was locked. Satisfied, she walked to the front of the shop, turned off the lights and closed the door behind her.

As she was inserting the key she suddenly turned around. She was sure someone was watching her. Looking around she saw no one, so she turned back around and locked the door.

Making sure she was not being followed she headed towards her house. As she made her way through Main Street a few people wished her luck on her date with Valentino.

She knew it. Gertrude did go see someone and told who ever it was that she was going on a date with Valentino. Oh boy, she was now in trouble. Yup, by tomorrow all of Wisterious Bay would know of her upcoming dinner date.

Guess that's what happens when you live in a small town.

Approaching her house, she couldn't help herself. She looked over at Valentino's house. Part of her was disappointed he wasn't outside or near any windows. The other part of her was glad because he still made her flush, and most importantly gave her butterflies in her stomach.

Closing the door behind her, she went directly to serve herself a glass of wine. It had been a long day and so much had happened she needed to sit and relax. However, the moment she served herself the glass Zoraida approached.

"Forgetting something?" Zoraida meowed her question.

"No. I haven't forgotten you. I just need two minutes and then I'll get you your meal," she replied looking at the kitten standing there before her.

If she didn't know any better, she'd think Zoraida waited for this precise moment to make an appearance. Mind you, not the moment she walked in the door or even after she took a sip of her wine. Nope, just as she was about to drink from her glass.

Zoraida watched Alicia as she took a sip.

"Por Dios. Esta bien. Vamos. Let's go," she couldn't help but smile.

Setting her wine glass down, she walked into the kitchen and retrieved a can from the cupboard. She opened it and placed the food in the bowl.

"There you go, enjoy. Todo bien?" she asked Zoraida.

Meow

"Oh, now you don't talk?" she shook her head.

"Your friends will be around soon enough to keep you company. Yo, me voy a bañar. See you after my bath," and with that Alicia climbed the stairs to her bedroom.

Knowing Felix and Augustus would be around soon and needing to speak with them about her suspicions she decided to bypass the bath and instead took a quick shower. Relaxed and dressed in comfortable pj's she descended the stairs and walked over to the fireplace.

After the fire was burning heartedly, she grabbed her wine glass and sat down in her favorite wing chair. Alicia picked up the book she'd been reading and before she knew it Felix and Augustus were clanking their way up the stairs.

"I see you started the party without us?" Felix the humorous one asked.

"Yes, I've had a long day and I needed to relax before you clowns invaded my space," she replied chuckling.

"Hey, I resent being called a clown. It's bad enough I was kicked out of a job and am no longer an official reaper, but a clown. That's where I draw the line," Augustus tried to sound upset.

Alicia knew Augustus wasn't really upset. He just liked to complain about everything. By now she was used to their antics.

"In all seriousness. I need your help," Alicia announced to all three.

"Of course. We're here to help. What do you need?" Felix was the first to answer and Augustus and Zoraida followed by nodding in agreement.

"I've uncovered who killed Sam. It was Dolores! Now, all I need is to figure out a way to make her confess. She's thinking of leaving town so it has to be done quickly. Any suggestions?" she asked.

They all started talking at the same time.

"Stop! One at a time guys. You're going to drive me crazy," she looked at Felix and nodded her head indicating he could go first.

"We can scare her into confessing," he stated rather proudly.

"Great idea, but if she doesn't then you've exposed yourself unnecessarily," Alicia replied.

"Can I go now?" Augustus asked.

"Yes, Augustus. What's your idea?" she asked.

"I could approach her first. She'll think death is here for her and I'll ask her if there's anything she wants to say or get off her chest before it's time to go. You'll be near by recording her response. And, then we have her right where we want her," Augustus stated. He couldn't actually smile, but Alicia imagined at that moment he was truly smiling.

Alicia remained silent for a moment while she thought it all out. Before saying anything, she wanted to know what Zoraida had to say.

"Well, no input from you?" she looked directly at the kitten.

"Me?" Zoraida replied as she licked her paw.

"Yes, you. What do you think we should do?" she replied.

"I like both their ideas. You can start off with Augustus appearing before her and if that doesn't work then Felix takes over. And, if that doesn't work, I'll talk to her. Either she'll tell the truth and confess or go crazy. Besides, who's going to believe her anyway?" Zoraida responded.

"Let me mull it over some. I'm liking the idea; I just want to make sure we do it right. We can't mess this up," she said to all three.

They nodded. She sat back up against her chair and closed her eyes running over the different possibilities in her head. Suddenly, she opened her eyes and sat straight up.

"It's a great idea. We're going to do exactly as Zoraida suggested. You all have to be inside. I'll stand under the window in the living room. Since everyone leaves their windows open during this time that part will be easy," she was liking more and more the idea of having them help her in making Dolores confess.

"So, when are we doing this?" Felix asked.

Turning to Zoraida she replied.

"Zoraida, necesito que tu, vayas a casa de Dolores. I need you to go over there and have a look around. Make sure she's not packing and planning on running out of town before we've had a chance to question her. Also, if she's acting strangely or appears dangerous get the heck out of there as fast as you can," she instructed Zoraida who leaped off her lap and jumped out the window.

"Well, while she's doing reconnaissance let us figure out the best time to approach her. I was thinking tomorrow," she said to both of them.

Before they could reply, she spoke.

"Oh, wait. We can't do it tomorrow. I have a dinner date. How about the next day?" she stated.

"An actual dinner date?" Felix asked.

"With whom?" Augustus inquired.

"An actual date as opposed to what? Anyway, guess the cat is out of the bag as they say. I might as well tell you now. Valentino stopped by the shop today and asked me out on a dinner date. I said yes and we're going out tomorrow night," she stated waiting for them to make some kind of sly remark.

Instead, she was quite surprised by their reaction.

"It's about time he asked you," Augustus said.

"Yep. About time," Felix added.

"Really?" she asked.

"He's a keeper. Besides, he's been thinking of asking you," Augustus stated.

"And, how do you know that?" Alicia was afraid to ask.

"Because we've been watching him. You know to make sure he was a good guy. And, he's been standing in front of the mirror practicing," Augustus moved back and forth as if he was laughing.

Felix on the other hand, clapped his hands.

Laughing Alicia nodded her head.

"You guys are too much. Anyway, so moving on. Since I'm going to dinner tomorrow, I don't want Valentino seeing us walking around the neighborhood outside. So, the following day it is," Alicia said to them both.

"If you're concerned, she may leave town, why don't we just plan on doing it late tomorrow night. Go to dinner early or change it for the next day," Augustus suggested.

Thinking it over she realized he was right. She thought about Dolores and her behavior and she was certain she'd be skipping town soon.

"You're right. I'll change my dinner plans for the following night and as soon as you guys are awake, we'll head over to Dolores' house," she informed them.

Just then Zoraida returned.

"That woman is crazier than you led me to believe," Zoraida said.

"What do you mean?" Alicia was worried Dolores would do something dangerous.

"She's pacing the room talking to herself. Something about a spell and she should have killed him sooner. Now, she'd have to leave town because no one else would help her," Zoraida replied.

"A spell? I wonder what she was talking about. Anyway, we've decided we're doing this tomorrow night. I'm going to work on a protection spell that will cover all four of us so that when we get to her house, she can't hurt us," Alicia announced.

"One of your spells?" Felix asked bringing his hand to his mouth.

"Yes! One of my spells. Why do you say it like that?" she asked.

"Because you know very well, your spells don't always come out as they intended and, on those occasions, God only knows what will happen," he replied clacking his mouth.

"Que cómico. You are just so hysterical," Alicia replied knowing quite well part of that statement was true.

There was never any guarantee her spells would work as they were intended. No matter how much she practiced. Sometimes she thought maybe there was something wrong with her. But her coven sisters and brothers all said not to give up.

That reminded her that she needed to stop by and visit Laura. There was something bothering her and if she could help then that's what coven sisters are for, to help each other out in times of need.

"Alright. So tomorrow night we pay Dolores a visit," she stated.

Everyone agreed.

"Now, I'm going into the kitchen to make myself a light dinner," she stood and headed towards the kitchen.

As she walked away, she could hear them arguing about exactly what to say to Dolores. She chuckled thinking of her peeps. They were just the best and she wouldn't trade them for anything in the world.

Grabbing a pan, she placed it on the stove and smiling started to gather ingredients. Oregano, Cumin, basil, and rosemary. Then she took out of the refrigerator a chicken breast that she had marinated the previous night. That had been seasoned with garlic, bijol, and mojo. *Que rico*, she thought to herself.

Just as she was about to place the chicken in the pan, there was a knock on the door. Startled as to who could be knocking this late, she ran into the living room and told everyone to hush. Satisfied they would remain silent she crept up to the door and looked through the peep hole. Sighing she yelled out.

"It's alright guys. It's only Meredith," she said out loud as she opened the door.

"Only Meredith? That's how you greet... tu prima? Que es eso?" Meredith laughed as she walked past her into the living.

"What's clanking guys?" she laughed even harder as she addressed Felix and Augustus unaware that Zoraida could speak.

"Well, good evening, Meredith," Zoraida said.

Meredith was so startled she jumped back, and inadvertently pushed Alicia down as they stumbled to the floor.

Looking from Alicia to Zoraida back to Alicia she asked.

"You have a talking cat?" she asked.

"Oh, yeah I forgot to tell you Zoraida apparently can speak," Alicia started laughing so hard she fell back onto Meredith who in turn started laughing so much she had tears in her eyes.

Chapter 12

After they had gotten off the floor and were back in the living room, and Meredith had stopped laughing, she said to Alicia.

"So, I've been waiting by my phone all night to hear from you and nothing? Nothing!" Meredith demanded.

"Was I supposed to call you?" Alicia was confused.

"YES! When you get invited to dinner by the hottest guy in Wisterious Bay, you have to tell your prima!" she said loudly.

"I didn't realize you knew already, my mistake," Alicia replied slapping her hand on her forehead.

"It doesn't matter. You should have called me the moment he left the shop to tell me cutie pie had invited you to dinner," she stated.

"Esta bien. It'll never happen again. What was I thinking?" Alicia chuckled.

"So, what are you wearing, when are you going? Where are you going" Meredith asked one question after another so rapidly Alicia just laughed.

"Por Dios mujer! Relax," Alicia chuckled.

"You know me. I'm nosy," Meredith replied smiling.

"Let's see... I don't know what I'm wearing. I haven't really had much time to think about it. I don't know where we are going or when," she replied keeping out the fact that she was going to suggest to Valentino they move up their dinner date to the following evening. She knew Meredith would try to talk her out of the idea.

"I thought dinner was for tomorrow night?" Meredith asked arching her eyebrows.

Sighing she replied.

"Yes, he asked me out for tomorrow night. It's just that something has come up and when he calls me, I'm going to suggest we move the dinner date for the following evening," Alicia replied knowing there was going to be a slew of questions.

Sure enough.

"What plans? What are you up to? What can be more important than going out to dinner with Mr. Hottie?" she rapidly asked the questions.

"You might as well know."

Before she could finish the question Meredith interrupted.

"Don't tell me you're going to be doing something dangerous?" she arched her eyebrows waiting for a response.

"No. I'll have Felix, Augustus, and Zoraida with me. I'll be perfectly safe," she replied as if having them as backup was natural.

"Stop right there. Dime todo, don't leave anything out. I want to know exactly what you're planning on doing tomorrow night," this time Meredith was serious.

"Well, if you must know. We're going to pay Dolores a visit to make her confess to the murder of Sam. I know she did it and I need her on the record so I can show Sheriff McDonald it was her who killed Sam," Alicia said waiting for Meredith's wrath.

"Are you insane? Estas loca?" she asked bringing her hands up to her head.

"No. Toda va a salir bien. Don't worry. I've got this covered," Alicia tried to sound as if she was in control. Part of her worried something would go wrong, but she trusted Felix, Augustus and now Zoraida to keep her safe.

"Well, there's no way you're going alone. I'm going to be right there next to you so explain to me exactly what you have planned so I'm in the loop," Meredith demanded.

All at once everyone started talking. Alicia looked at Meredith and shrugged.

By the time the plan had been explained to Meredith the only thing she added was that she'd bring some of her special tea. She would tell Dolores it was their way of paying their condolences. That would get them in the door and Alicia wouldn't have to be hiding under the window.

They agreed to the time. Once Meredith arrived and Alicia had her phone ready to record, they'd head out to Dolores' house.

Meredith sat in the kitchen while Alicia made dinner. She'd added another chicken breast and made a salad for both of them. Once dinner was served, they sat down at talked about what else was going on in town. One thing that was bothering Meredith was Laura's behavior lately.

"You noticed it also?" Alicia asked.

"Yes. It's strange. She's acting as if she'd switch a light and was now another person. Never has she missed a morning coffee with us. When I stopped by her shop to ask if everything was alright. She dismissed me apologizing she was so busy she totally forgot and said she joined us soon. Soon! What does that mean?" Meredith stated rather confused.

"You know we really don't know that much about her. For the most part she's been rather reserved about her past and her family. I'm wondering if this has something to do with a family member, we know nothing about? Maybe she's just overwhelmed and doesn't want to burden us with her problems. We need to make a point of just telling her tomorrow if she shows up at the Cauldron that we're here to support her in any way she needs," Alicia stated.

"Perfecto. I agree. Let's see if she shows up tomorrow. If not, I'd wait until our next coven meeting in a few days and see if she's better. She probably just needed some time to herself," Meredith added.

Meredith stayed a while longer after dinner. She wanted to try and beat Felix in chess. Unsuccessful after three tries, she gave up and bid goodnight to everyone. As she walked out the door, she reminded Alicia to not leave without her tomorrow night, and that she'd see her first thing in the morning for coffee.

The next morning Alicia woke earlier than usual. She showered and was ready to head out the door as soon as she fed Zoraida.

"Now behave today. I'm going to stop by the shop and drop off these herbs at the lab and then to breakfast with Meredith and Laura. If anything, unusual comes up come and find me. But for all that is holy do not under any circumstances speak to me. I don't want anyone to accidentally overhear you speaking," she stated.

"What do you think I was born yesterday?" she replied and walked over to her bowl ignoring Alicia.

Alicia grabbed her jacket as the temperature had dropped a few degrees and headed out the door. Walking on Main Street during this time of year was invigorating. The changing of trees, the colorful decorations in town, and the vibe one felt walking around Wisterious Bay was just what she needed to start the day.

Her purse buzzed indicating a text. She wondered who'd be sending her a text so early in the morning. Retrieving the phone from her purse she read.

Good morning, Alicia, Sebastian here just letting you know that once Lotions & Things Boutique has relinquished their key, I have already scheduled for the contractor to come in assess anything that we may have to take care of and they'll be painting the walls. I'll need you to tell me if you have a preference in color.

Relinquishing the key? What was he talking about? Dialing his number, she waited until the second ring when he answered.

"Good morning, Alicia. You didn't have to call me back right away. You could have just sent me a text the color you wanted the walls painted," he stated.

"What are you talking about? I'm totally confused," she replied.

"I'm sorry. I was told you were aware that Lotions & Things has asked to terminate their lease effective immediately," he stated.

"Why is Laura closing shop? Is she leaving town?" Alicia asked.

"I don't have any specifics as to the why. She just sent us a formal thirty-day notice stating she was terminating the lease. And, as to her leaving town? She didn't explain the reason why she was terminating her lease, just that she was closing shop," he responded.

"That's so weird. She'd been acting rather distant these last few days. Meredith and I were planning on asking her about it or at least letting her know we were there if she needed us, but I never imagined she'd be doing any of this and especially leaving town," Alicia sounded worried.

"Well, then how would you like us to handle this situation?" he asked.

"Hold off on doing anything until I've had a chance to speak with her. Give me a few days and I'll call you," Alicia informed Sebastian.

"Sounds good. I'll await your instructions. By the way, how's the business going? I see you've had a stellar month so far from Patchouli Mystical Tesoros," he stated.

"It's been amazing. The shop is doing great. Inventory is selling like crazy, and I expect by the end of the end another record quarter," she replied smiling.

At first, when she moved into town, she was worried inheriting her father's estate she would blunder it or somehow make a huge mess of things. But with the help of Sebastian and the law firm she's made a huge profit.

"Well, keep up the great work. And, remember if you ever need me, I'm a ring away," he said and with that he hung up the phone.

Alicia placed her phone back in her purse and continued her walk. As she approached the back of the shop, she noticed someone running away. It looked as if they had been at her back door.

"STOP!" she screamed.

The person running stopped for an instant and then took off running. Alicia knew they had heard her, but decided it was too risky to follow. Instead, she looked around and feeling it was safe, she continued to the door. When she tried the handle, the door opened.

Immediately, she realized someone had entered her shop. *But how*, she thought to herself. There was no force entry. Slowly opening the door, she called out. If anyone is in here, I've already called the police.

"Come out now and I'll cancel the call," she yelled out.

Of course, no one answered. So, she walked in and turned on the lights. Looking around she didn't see anything had been disturbed.

Nothing was out of place. When she went into her office, there is where she found the mess. Every inch of her office had been turned upside down. Papers were thrown all over the floor, cabinets were emptied, and even drawers were removed from the hinges.

Someone had deliberately gone into her office looking for something. Closing her eyes, she said a spell out loud to see if the intruder would be revealed to her. Nothing. Her magic never worked when she needed it the most. Knowing she had no choice she took out her phone and dialed 911.

"Where's your emergency," the caller stated.

"Hi, Bertha. It's me Alicia. I need to report a break-in at The Patchouli Mystical Tesoros Shop," she sounded drained.

"Oh honey, are you alright?" Bertha asked.

"Yes. I'm fine. It's just my office. Someone was in here looking for God knows what. As I approached the back door to the shop just now, I noticed someone running away. I couldn't make out who it was, so I can't give you a description. I'm sorry," Alicia stated.

"No worries. Sheriff McDonald just walked into the station, so I'll send him over right away," Bertha replied.

"Great, thanks," Alicia responded wishing it had been anyone else except him.

Knowing she wasn't supposed to touch anything she left her office and walked outside. She remembered she'd use her hand to open the door, but her fingerprints would be there anyway so she wasn't worried. A few minutes later Sheriff McDonald drove up the alleyway and parked the police cruiser. Stepping out of the vehicle he just nodded.

"Do you get up every morning thinking of ways to make my life miserable?" he asked as he approached her.

"Yes. That's my only goal in life?" Alicia stated while placing her hands on her hips.

"Don't be smart with me," McDonald demanded.

"Well, you started it," she again placed her hands on her hips.

"How old are we again? Never mind, don't answer that. Just tell me what happened," he said trying to be the better person.

Alicia went through everything she remembered from the moment she walked around the back of the shop including seeing someone running away. She then pushed the back door she'd left pried open with a rock. After Sheriff McDonald walked inside, she followed.

Taking him to her office she told him she'd check everything else and the only thing that was disturbed was her office.

Looking around he asked her if she thought of who could have broken in or what they were looking for?

"That's the thing. First of all, I'm not even sure how they got in. There was no forced entry, yet no one except Gertrude and I have a key to the shop. Secondly, nothing was stolen not even the little money we keep in the register. So, whatever they were looking for was in the office. The problem is I can't think of anything they'd want from there," and just as she said those last words it dawned on her. She knew exactly what they were looking for.

By the time Sheriff McDonald left Gertrude had arrived. Alicia decided to keep the shop closed for the day. They put up a sign that said family emergency and that they'd be open the next day. Alicia sent Gertrude home and she walked over to the Cauldron where Meredith was waiting.

She briefly told her what had happened and that she was going to take her coffee to go and then she asked Meredith if she'd go back with her to the shop. She wanted to check something out.

Agreeing they returned to the shop and entered through the back. Alicia explained the only thing that someone would break into the shop for if not the merchandise was the spell book.

Alicia hurriedly went to the secret wall and pushed it open. After turning on the lights took two stairs at a time until she reached the bottom. Running to where she hid the book and was relieved to see it was still there.

"Is it still there?" Meredith asked.

"Yes. I have an invisibility spell on it so that if someone comes close to it, they can't see it. But yes, it's still here," she replied grateful no one had taken her family's spell book.

"Do you really think that's what they were after?" Meredith asked.

"It's the only explanation. The person I saw running must have been Dolores. Now more than ever we need to confront her tonight. This has gotten out of hand and we need to stop this before someone else gets hurt," now Alicia was getting angry.

"I agree. Go home and relax the rest of the day. I'm going to the shop and telling the girls I need them to work it alone today and then I'll head over to your place," Meredith stated as she ushered Alicia towards the stairs.

"You're right. Let's go. This will be over soon," Alicia said as she turned off the lights and closed the wall securely.

Outside they hugged.

"Te veo después," Alicia said.

"See you later," Meredith responded the same.

By the time that Alicia had arrived home she was angrier than she wanted to be.

"What is wrong with you?" Zoraida asked as she slammed the door.

"The nerve of that woman. Who does she think she is? First, she kills Sam and now she's breaking into my shop to steal my family's spell book," Alicia said at the top of her lungs.

Zoraida figured if she remained quiet, she'd get the whole story.

"And, how did she even know about the spell book in the first place?" she demanded.

After a few seconds of not saying anything, Zoraida spoke.

"Did she find the spell book?"

"No! If she'd stolen my spell book, I would've killed her," she said those words with such rage they even startled her.

Zoraida knew her enough now to know that she'd never kill anyone. Just at that moment there was a knock on the door. Alicia tried to ignore bit, but the knock continued. Walking over to the door ready to scream at whomever was making that ruckus she opened the door with such force she stumbled back.

"Oh dear. Are you alright?" Haydee said as she stood there shocked.

"Oh, Haydee. I'm so sorry. I had no idea it was you knocking. Please do come in," she moved out the way indicating for Haydee to come inside.

"Are you sure? I only came by to see if you were alright as you're never home during the day," she stated.

Alicia sat down in a chair and covered her face with her hands. Haydee immediately went over to her and put her hand on her back.

"It's alright. Tell me what's going on," she said gently.

Between sobs Alicia told her about the break-in. She didn't say anything about the spell book. Instead, she said she couldn't figure out why would anyone want to break into her shop and destroy her office and not take any of the merchandise or even the money.

"It's obvious they were looking for something. The most important thing is you are safe. I'm going to go into the kitchen and make you some tea. I'll find what I need. You sit here and relax," she said as she walked towards the kitchen.

At this time, Zoraida approached Alicia. She rubbed her body against her leg and purred. Then looked up at Alicia and whispered.

"If you haven't figured it out yet. Haydee's a witch. You can trust her. If you tell her what's really going on she might be able to help," she suggested.

"I know she's a witch. Although she's never attended any of our coven meetings. But I just don't want anything to happen to her and Dolores is out of control. I can't risk putting Haydee in danger," she replied.

"What danger?" Haydee asked as she returned with a steaming cup of tea.

Alicia looked at Zoraida who nodded.

"I actually believe I know who broke into my shop," she said as she took the cup from Haydee.

"Who?" she asked.

"Dolores! She killed Sam and now she's after something I hold dear to me. But I've got this covered. Tomorrow Meredith and I are exposing her for the killer she is and then Wisterious Bay will go back to being the peaceful town it's always been," she stated.

Haydee had seen it. Something big was brewing and Sam's death was just the beginning. Before all Hollow's Eve there would be another murder. Haydee decided she didn't need to overwhelm Alicia any more than she was already, so she kept that bit of detail to herself.

Chapter 13

Meredith had shown up shortly after Haydee had departed and stayed until it was time to visit Dolores. Once Felix and Augustus were ready, she called out to Zoraida and armed with a fully charged cell phone and a protection spell they headed out the door.

Felix and Augustus swerved in and out of backyards as to avoid being seen by anyone. Every once in a while, Felix made such a clutter Alicia was sure someone would see him. But every time Zoraida came to the rescue and anyone looking only saw a kitten roaming around the street instead of a walking and talking skeleton.

Augustus was able to float which made it easier for him to hide when needed. As they arrived at Dolores's house, they all noticed she had every single light turned on. At first, they thought maybe she had company. But after Zoraida walked around the perimeter inspecting every inch of the house, and glancing in some of the windows, she realized the house was very quiet.

"Are you ready?" Meredith asked.

Looking at Zoraida to confirm before responding she was confused as to what she was saying.

"Wait there's no one there?" Alicia asked.

"That's not what I'm saying. From looking in some of the windows it appeared as if no one was home. That doesn't mean Dolores is not in one of the rooms. All that means is that the house is *not* full of people," Zoraida replied.

Nodding she looked at Meredith and told her even though she wasn't really ready they needed to get this over with so she could then call Sheriff McDonald and end this nightmare.

"Here goes nothing," Meredith said as she knocked.

After a few minutes of no one answering the door Meredith looked at Alicia and shrugging her shoulders tried to see if the door would open.

"What are you doing?" Alicia whispered.

"We might as well see if she's home and if not, maybe we can find some evidence," Meredith said as she slowly pushed the door open.

"Are you insane? We can go to jail. You do know this is breaking and entering right?" she tried to pull Meredith back.

Pushing her arm away Meredith walked into the foyer waving at Alicia to follow. Looking around to make sure no one was outside; Alicia entered the house saying a little prayer that they'd not get caught.

She had turned to close the door when she heard a scream. Turning back around quickly she noticed Meredith had covered her mouth with her hands.

"Why are you screaming. Do you want us to get caught?" she whispered getting angry at Meredith's behavior.

She arched her eyebrows and pointed into what Alicia figured was the living room. Approaching slowly, she immediately realized why Meredith had screamed.

There in the living room lay Dolores obviously dead.

"Oh no, not again! This can't be happening. What do we do now?" Alicia's mind was reeling.

"The first thing we need to do is send your peeps home. They can't be here when Sheriff McDonald arrives," she stated rather sternly.

"You're right," she said as she walked outside to look for Felix and Augustus. Zoraida followed.

When she spotted them behind the tree she approached and whispering told them they had just found Dolores dead and they needed to head home right away. She would be calling Sheriff McDonald soon and they needed to get out of there before everyone showed up.

Agreeing they left, but Zoraida told her she'd stay behind just in case she needed anything.

"By the way, you need to do a protection spell right away before you walk back into that house. I didn't want to tell you anything, but there's some bad vibe in that house," Zoraida told Alicia.

"Thank you. I'll do that right now," Alicia said as she closed her eyes and said a silent incantation.

Walking back inside the house she found Meredith standing exactly where she had left her.

"I guess you decided to wait for me to investigate?" she asked.

"Heck yeah. You're the sleuth. I prefer to work in the background especially since my magic has not been working lately," Meredith replied.

"About that, have you spoken to Laura or any of the coven members to figure out what's going on in that department?" she inquired.

"No, I've been so busy and besides that, Laura has been MIA all this time that I just haven't gotten around to discussing it with anyone. I'm sure it's nothing, but I promise I'll talk to someone in the coven to see if they've seen this before or if they have any suggestions on what I should do to rectify the matter," she told Alicia.

"Good. Now that that's settled let's see if we can pick up any clues before call the police station," Alicia said as she looked around.

"Por Dios. Do you see what I'm seeing?" Meredith stood over the body startled.

"What?" Alicia was still looking around the room and hadn't focus too much on the body.

"The knife that's sticking out of her back is from your kitchen at The Patchouli Mystical Tesoros Shop," she stated

"No es posible! There's no way! It's impossible," she shook her head.

"Look, it's from your set. Besides, I would know. I gave you that set when you first opened the shop," she replied.

"This does not look good. Ahora que ago?" she said out loud.

"What you do now is make sure not to touch anything. I'm going to call 911 and I'll do all the talking," Meredith instructed.

"Alright," Alicia answered.

Just as Meredith took out her cell phone to call the police Alicia stopped her.

"You know what this means right? That Dolores can't possibly have been the killer. That puts us back to square one. Now, we have to figure out not only who killed Sam, but who killed Dolores. Could it be the same person and if so, why?" Alicia said.

"That's the one-thousand-dollar question. Why?" Meredith shrugged as she dialed the phone.

"Where's your emergency?"

"This is Meredith, I'm at Dolores's house and someone killed her. I need Sheriff McDonald to come over immediately," she said into the receiver.

"First Alicia, now you. You gals sure do seem to find yourselves in quite a predicament. Anyway, I've just notified Sheriff McDonald and the coroner's office. Everyone should be there shortly," she replied.

While Meredith put her phone away, she thought how true those words were. It seemed as hard as she tried, she always ended up in the thick of things right along side Alicia.

Alicia had been walking around the room taking pictures when Meredith interrupted her thoughts.

"Oye, listen. Vamos. Let's go outside and wait for everyone by the door. There's nothing else here that can give us a hint as to what happened except for the obvious and we want to stay out of McDonald's way. You know the moment he realizes you're involved he's going to get very angry," Meredith said as she pushed Alicia towards the front door.

She was right. Alicia needed to brace herself for what was coming.

Two minutes later two cars approached with sirens and flashing lights.

"Here comes the calvary," Alicia whispered to her cousin.

"Prima, it's going to be fine," Meredith replied.

Getting out of the cruiser, Alicia could tell Sheriff McDonald was in a foul mood.

"Another murder Alicia. You couldn't settle for one, no you had to have two murders?" he demanded.

"Me? I'm an innocent bystander. I had nothing to do with Sam's death or Dolores for that matter," she tried to sound determined.

Instead, she came across unsure.

"I know these murders have something to do with you. You better watch your back as I'm going to solve this mystery, and if I find that you had anything to do with this case, even the most minuscule indication, I'm going to arrest you and throw away the key. Is that clearly understood?" he demanded.

"Si," she replied trying to not say anything that would incriminate her.

"Don't *si* me Missy. Just agree to the fact that you will stay out of this case and out of my way," he growled.

"Fine," she replied as she put her hands on her hip.

Sheriff McDonald was starting to feel like a thorn in her side. The last thing she wanted was for him to arrest her. It was bad enough already that he thought she was the number one suspect. Now, with this new murder things were going to get very dicey for Alicia.

After walking around the body and doing a preliminary check, Sheriff McDonald returned to where Alicia was standing.

"So, tell me what happened here?" he asked Alicia with a frown on his face and a heavy sigh.

"Let me start by saying I had nothing to do with this. To be perfectly clear I didn't kill Dolores or Sam for that matter," Alicia said.

"I'll be the judge of that, but for now just tell me what happened here from the moment you arrived. Don't leave any details out!" he demanded.

"Fine. Meredith and I stopped by with some tea from her shop, Hannah Tea House..."

Before she could continue, he interrupted her.

"Do you take me for a fool? I know Meredith owns a tea shop. I also know the name of the shop. Now, tell me what happened or I'm arresting you for obstruction," he now actually growled.

Alicia figured she had pushed enough and without mentioning Felix, Augustus or Zoraida told him what happened since they arrived.

"Well, you did say leave nothing out. But I'll start again," she needed to dig just a little further.

He annoyed her so much any opportunity to frustrate him was a pleasure.

"So, we approached the porch and knocked. As a matter of fact, we knocked several times and we didn't hear anything. Suddenly, we heard what sounded like a thump," she said as she looked at them.

Now, she was lying. But she couldn't actually tell him they'd just decided to snoop around and that seemed like the most logical story.

"We called out and still no response so Meredith tried the door. When it opened, we walked in and called out to Dolores to see if she was alright or if she needed help. Obviously, we got no response," Alicia stated.

"When did you decide to walk into the house?" he asked suspiciously.

"After we opened the door, we walked into the foyer and Meredith moving ahead of me to let me in is how she found Dolores lying there in the living room. She screamed and that's when I moved in closer and saw the body," Alicia concluded.

She was not about to tell him they'd realize the knife used to kill Dolores was from her shop's kitchen. Sheriff McDonald would figure it out soon enough and at that point she'd hopefully come up with the name of the killer. For now, she kept that part out of the equation.

"There's something you're not telling me. You better not be withholding information. Because if I find out you'd kept pertinent details that could help this case, I'm not going to respond so kindly," he said looking directly at Alicia.

All she did was stare back at him hoping he couldn't tell how nervous she was.

"Are we good here?" she asked hoping they were dismissed.

"For now. Do not leave town and be available if I need to call you for more questions. You and your cousin are free to go," he waved his hand around dismissing her.

That was fine with her. Alicia turned around and walked over to Meredith who was in the foyer talking to one of the police officers. She waited patiently until Meredith was dismissed and they both walked out of the house without saying a word.

The moment they walked in the door Felix and Augustus were waiting in the foyer ready to bombard her with questions.

"Before you both say anything, Meredith and I found Dolores dead. That means that the real killer is lose somewhere here in Wisterious Bay, and I've been wrong all along. We have to start from scratch and figure out who killed Sam and is Dolores's killer the same person or are we dealing with two killers. And, we have to do this NOW because otherwise Sheriff McDonald will surely arrest me," Alicia waved them away stopping them from asking any questions as she made her way towards the kitchen.

That didn't stop them, they just pounded Meredith for answers.

"Follow me," she said laughing.

She yelled out to Alicia to bring her a glass of wine and sat down to tell them what little she knew. By the time that Alicia had changed and returned with two glasses, Felix was playing a game of chess with Meredith. Augustus was watching the game, and Zoraida was sleeping by the bay window.

"Prima, I forgot to ask you. What did you finally say to Valentino when you told him you couldn't meet him tonight?" she asked.

"You know, if I hadn't changed plans with him, we never would've found Dolores and had to deal with Sheriff McDonald," she rolled her eyes.

"Well, knowing you the dinner date would have been a total flop because you would have spent the entire evening thinking about Dolores," Meredith replied.

"You're right. Anyway, he said it would not be a problem that actually it turned out perfect because he had to do something and had forgotten all about it. So, it worked out well all around," she stated.

"Did he tell you what was so urgent he had to *do it* tonight and not another night?" Meredith asked

"No, but I didn't press him for an answer. I figured it was work or who knows what. Why do you think I should have asked him?" she now wondered.

"Just interesting that he was going to reschedule on the night that Dolores was killed. You don't find that interesting?" Meredith raised her eyebrows.

"Noooo. You don't think he's the killer, do you?" Alicia was now wondering.

"Well, we do have to start all over again from the beginning. You yourself said there could be one or two killers and everyone you suspected before is now a suspect again. That includes me," she looked at Alicia waiting for a response.

"Por favor! You're not a suspect," she said looking down and avoiding making eye contact as she had at one point considered even if just for a brief moment that she might be a killer. But she'd never admit that to her and hurt her feelings.

"Yeah, whatever. Anyway, let me help you figure out this case. I don't want anyone else getting killed, and that includes us," she said.

"That'd be great. Let me get my list and you can help me fill in the gaps," Alicia said as she went to her office to retrieve her handwritten list. The one on the phone had comments about Meredith and she didn't want her to see that one.

She returned and set everything down on the dining room table. They got to work and before they realized it, they'd been working nonstop for over an hour. Stretching Alicia got up and asked Meredith if she was hungry.

"Si, claro!" she chuckled.

"I figured as much. Let me make something quick for us and then we can call it a night. We'll look over all of this tomorrow, but for tonight I'm done," Alicia yawned again.

"Sounds like a plan. While you're whipping something yummy for us to eat, I'm going to see if I can get in another game with Felix. I refuse to give up. Sooner or later, I will beat him at chess," she walked out of the dining room in search of Felix who undoubtedly was by the fireplace playing a game with Augustus who appeared less than thrilled at the moment.

"You're cheating!" Augustus stomped his scythe hard on the wooden floors.

"You're just a sore loser!" Felix yelled back as his bones made loud clacking noise.

"I'll..."

"Stop this right now you two!" Meredith tried to be louder than them.

They just looked at her and completely ignoring her went to back to their banter.

"Well, I guess I won't be playing any chess today," she said making it seem as if she was leaving.

"Wait!" Felix replied.

Looking over at Augustus he tilted his skeletal head towards Meredith.

"Fine. I'm done for the night anyway," Augustus answered and left in search of Alicia.

Satisfied, Felix moved his arm indicating for Meredith to take a seat at the table. Smiling she nodded and complied with his request thinking this is the day I'm beating Felix.

That game didn't last long.

"Check Mate," Felix said and clapped his hands.

"You like to gloat, don't you?" Meredith threw her arms in the air surrendering.

Felix just laughed.

At that moment Alicia yelled out.

"Food's ready. Come serve yourself."

"Be right there," Meredith replied.

Once they had their food and their glasses of wine replenished, they moved back into where Felix and Zoraida were resting. Alicia told Meredith she'd only put two logs in the fireplace as it was late. She then sat in her favorite wing chair and for the rest of the night they talked about everything except Dolores and the murder investigation.

"So, are you excited about going to dinner with Valentino?" Meredith asked.

"Yes, unless he's the killer," she laughed.

Chapter 14

The next day Alicia left home and headed toward The Cauldron Coffee House hoping that Laura would show up early. She was starting to get worried about her. Besides she wanted to see if she could speak with her in private about what Sebastian had said.

As she walked past Lotions & Things Boutique, she noticed Laura was inside with her back to the window. She walked up to the glass door and knocked. Turning around and not having much of a choice, Laura took a deep breath and walked over to the door and unlocked it.

"Alicia, what can I do for you?" Laura stood with the door only partially open.

"You're not going to let me in?" Alicia asked.

"Sorry, of course. Come in," Laura replied as she opened the door further.

"I've been worried about you and I wanted to make sure everything was alright. And if not, if there was anything I could do to help you," Alicia stated.

"Everything is fine. Sorry, I've been so non-responsive. It's just that there is a lot going on and I haven't had time to attend our morning coffee get together," she replied hoping Alicia would drop it.

Sure, enough she didn't.

"Well, it's obvious something is going on. I hope you'll trust me enough to let me help you," she said waiting to see if Laura would confide in her.

"Seriously, I'm taking care of it. Soon, everything will be as it should be," she replied.

Alicia wasn't sure what that meant, and since it was evident that Laura didn't want to share with her whatever was bothering her, she dropped it.

"There's another matter I wanted to discuss with you. I received a call from my lawyer and he informed me you want to break the lease on Lotions & Things Boutique. Is that true?" she inquired.

"Yes, as I mentioned in our last coven meeting. It's time for me to move on. I've been meaning to travel for a while and what better time than the present. I just have to finish one last thing before I can leave," she stated.

"I wish you weren't leaving us. Is there any way I can convince you to stay?" Alicia asked.

"No! She answered without hesitation.

"I'm sorry to hear that. I really wish you'd reconsider," Alicia asked again.

Changing the subject Laura breathed in deeply and continued.

"So, to answer your other question, yes. I contacted Mr. Sunbean and informed him I wanted to break the lease. I'm sure you'll have no problem finding someone new right away. It's always been a prime location," she said dismissing Alicia.

"I guess I can have him start looking for a new tenant," Alicia replied.

"As a matter of fact, I know a few of our coven sisters would be interested in either starting their own business or possibly taking over my shop. If that's the case then you don't have to worry about the lease. We can just transfer it to them," Laura said looking directly into Alicia's eyes so intently she had to look away.

To Alicia, Laura seemed angry. However, she couldn't fathom what would have her behaving this way. She figured it was time to drop it. Changing the subject, she asked if Laura was joining them this morning for coffee.

Thinking it over she agreed.

"Great, we can walk together," Alicia smiled.

Not budging Laura figured she might as well join her. Otherwise, she'd never be able to get rid of her.

"Sure. I can spare a half an hour to join you and Meredith. Let me finish a couple of things here and I'll join you," Laura replied.

"Oh, no worries. I'll just wait for you," Alicia moving over to stand by the front door.

"Well, in that case why don't we just head over there now?" Laura gave up trying to dissuade Alicia from hanging around.

"Are you sure?" Alicia asked knowing quite well that Laura had been trying to get rid of her.

"Yes. Of course. Let's head out," she said as she grabbed the keys.

Alicia walked out the door and Laura was tempted to lock her out, but decided against it. She didn't need Alicia thinking she was crazy. So, she walked out, locked the door to the shop, and they walked together to The Cauldron Coffee House.

When they arrived, Alicia realized Meredith wasn't due for another few minutes so she ordered coffee for the table and they sat down to wait.

"I've been meaning to ask you Laura. Do you have family?" Alicia inquired.

"What kind of question is that? Of course, I have family," she looked at Alicia as if she had grown two horns.

"It's just that you never really talk about them and I was curious," she replied.

"Did you ever hear that saying - curiosity killed the cat - well, you should think about it. It's popular for a reason," Laura answered narrowing her eyes at Alicia.

In that instant Alicia felt such a powerful negative surge she was shocked. At that moment Meredith walked up to the table.

"Laura, you're here. I'm so glad to see you. We'd been so worried about you," she said as she leaned in for a hug.

Laura stiffened, but immediately relaxed and hugged Meredith back patting her on her back.

Sitting down Meredith didn't notice the tension between Laura and Alicia. The waitress at this point had followed Meredith to the table, and even if she'd notice she wouldn't have said anything at that moment. They were asked if they wanted the usual.

"Yes," they answered in unison.

Once the waitress had left Meredith asked Laura about the upcoming festivities. She answered monotonously. Meredith looked at Alicia as she shrugged in response.

Then suddenly Laura's mood swing changed. She was chatty and even laughing. Old Laura was back Meredith thought to herself. Alicia wasn't so sure, but didn't say anything to aggravate Laura.

By the time they finished breakfast Alicia was anxiously waiting to speak with Meredith alone. Shortly after, Laura excused herself saying she needed to get back to the shop to get some things done before she opened the shop for the day.

"How are you doing with inventory? I'm starting to sell out and will need to make a new batch in a few days," Alicia said to both.

"I'm fine for now," Meredith replied.

Laura seemed to be thinking. When she looked up and realized they were both waiting for an answer she cleared her throat.

"Sorry, I'm working on something new and I should have everything I need in the next few days," Laura answered.

"Oh, that sounds exciting. Can you share with us your secret?" Meredith asked.

"No! All in good time, all in good time," she replied and smiled one of those smiles that never reached the side of your face. Those types of smiles that were strained and forced.

"Well, I can't wait to see what happens next," Alicia smiled.

"Oh, you'll all be surprised, that's for certain," Laura replied and with that stood. She placed some money on that table to cover per portion of the bill and bid them a good day. She then exited The Cauldron Coffee House, but before leaving she stopped at the door and turned around to look directly at Alicia.

"Prima, am I imagining it or is Laura acting really strange? She was acting as if she was mad at me," Alicia stated.

"No way. There's no reason for her to be mad at you. I'm sure whatever is going on is personal and has nothing to do with you," Meredith replied.

Alicia remained pensive. When the waitress brought their check, Meredith gave her a credit card and announced to Alicia she'd cover her portion. Alicia thanked her for breakfast and once again fell silent. As they waited, they both remained lost in their thoughts. After Meredith added tip and signed, they stood and exited the coffee house.

"Te veo después," Meredith said to Alicia.

"Hasta luego prima," she replied.

They hugged and each headed towards their own shop. Alicia was so busy all day with customers that by the time it was closing she was exhausted. Looking at her watch she asked Gertrude to close up shop because she needed to get ready for her dinner date.

"Good luck tonight. I'm sure you and Valentino are going to hit it off," she smiled and waved at Alicia as she walked out the door.

A bit nervous and wondering why she had agreed to the dinner date in the first place Alicia picked two outfits and went back and forth deciding until Zoraida had enough and told her which option she needed to pick.

Satisfied with the suggestion, she took a quick shower, finished getting dressed, and put on a little makeup. By the time Valentino arrived to pick her up for dinner, she was a nervous wrecking ball.

"You look amazing tonight," Valentino said as he stood in her doorway.

"Thank you," she replied blushing.

The rest of the night they spent talking about quirky family members, townspeople, odd jobs, and of course magic.

"So, did you always know you were a warlock?" Alicia asked him.

"Yes. I was very lucky that I had a tutor that showed me the right way to do my magic. I could have easily gone into dark magic, but it never felt right. I'm happy where I am and my magic has served me well," he replied smiling.

"Is there a reason Gertrude doesn't know about what you can do?" she asked.

"She knows. She just chooses to ignore it and will have nothing to do with magic. So, I respect her wishes and act as if she knows nothing about it. It works well for both of us," he replied.

"Wait. You're telling me she knows you're a warlock?" she stated.

He nodded his response.

"Then that means she knows I'm a witch," Alicia said more to herself.

"Probably. Although she's never mentioned it to me. She doesn't mind working in the thick of it as they say, she just doesn't want anything to do with magic itself," he replied.

"All these years and I never knew. Don't worry, I won't mention anything to her, promise. I'll even continue acting the same way I have been all along. But I am curious as to why she doesn't want anything to do with magic?" Alicia asked Valentino.

"Thank you. As to your question, she's never told me the truth. However, I suspect it has something to do with Sam. From what I recall he used to dabble in magic back in the day when he lived here in Wisterious Bay," he replied.

"What? You mean to tell me Sam? No way," she said without finishing her sentence.

"From what I remember they were more parlor tricks than real magic. But he's always had a fascination with magic. I'm assuming he must have been showing off like he always did and something happened. From that day on, Gertrude stayed away from anything she thought was actual magic," he answered.

"Interesting. Maybe someday she'll tell us what really happened. Magic is not all bad. Well, that is unless your me and sometimes blunder my spells," Alicia laughed.

"So, do tell more," Valentino chuckled.

Just then their main meal came. By the time they had finished and ordered dessert they resumed their conversation.

"Do you think the coven will survive now that Laura has decided to move out of Wisterious Bay?" Alicia asked.

"I don't really know anyone in the coven. It would depend if there's someone interested in taking on the role of leader. Or unless someone has already been assigned," he responded.

"To tell you the truth, I'm not certain. I've been attending the meetings sporadically because sometimes my shop gets so busy, I've stayed opened way past closing. Other times I've needed to replenish my inventory," she pondered.

"Well, it'll be interesting to see how this plays out. But back to your blunder, do tell," Valentino laughed.

"Very funny. Fine. Let's see which one is the least embarrassing. Oh yeah, I was conjuring a new spell that I wrote down only to have it literally blow up in my face. I lost part of my eyebrow, a few eyelashes and singed the front of my hair. I looked like a crazy witch. Como una loca," she flushed.

"Oh my, I'm trying not to laugh at you, but the image that popped up as you were describing what happened was just too funny. I'm sorry," Valentino cringed his face as if trying to say I'm sorry without actually saying the words out loud.

"I know, I know. Most of the time my spells do come out fine. It's just every once in a while, something happens and then poof, it goes haywire." Alicia smiled rather embarrassed.

"Back up a minute. What does como una loca mean? Is that Spanish?" Valentino asked.

"Oh yeah, sorry I forgot you don't understand. Yes, it's Spanish and it means like a crazy person. I was just saying that's what I looked like that day when my spell blew up in my face. It was not a pretty sight."

Now she chuckled.

Laughing Valentino reached across the table and placed his hand on top of hers. At that moment an electrical charged passed through them so strong they both recoiled. For a moment they looked at each other and no words escaped either of them. Then Valentino looked up and saw the waiter heading their way.

"Oh, look dessert is here," Valentino said breaking the ice.

They ate in silence each lost in their thoughts trying to figure out what that surge had meant. Neither wanting to dwell too much on the matter, did not speak of it again.

When they were done, Valentino offered to walk her back to her house. Glad to have changed the subject Alicia agreed.

Walking down Main Street Alicia pointed out several of the local stores. Telling him about each of the proprietors, how long they'd been in business and a little bit about each of them.

By the time they reached Alicia's house they had forgotten all about the electrical surged that had passed between them.

"Thank you for lovely evening. I had a wonderful time," Alicia said feeling more and more comfortable around him.

The butterflies were there, just not as bad. At least now she could have a conversation with him without blubbering some ridiculous statement that would make her appear inept.

"I'm glad you agreed to having dinner with me. I've wanted to ask you since the very first day I saw you at the bakery," Valentino said looking directly into her eyes.

Now she blushed again.

"Aw, it was a great evening," Alicia didn't know what else to say so she just smiled.

Looking up at her window she could see Felix, Augustus, and Zoraida at the window watching them. Felix was clapping and Augustus was stomping his scythe.

"Do you hear that sound? It's like thump, thump," Valentino said as he looked around.

Alicia's familiars all scrambled away from the window just as Valentino looked their way.

"Nope. I don't hear a thing," Alicia replied hoping against all odds he didn't see them in the window. *Por Dios they are going to be the death of me*, Alicia thought to herself as she turned Valentino around and patted him on the shoulder.

"Well, this has been fun. We should do this again," and with that she ran inside to scold Felix and Augustus not realizing Zoraida was the instigator.

"I'll call you?" he yelled out as she closed the door.

Shrugging he walked home. Before opening the door, he looked one more time next door and smiled. *She definitely was interesting*, he thought as he entered the house.

"What were you guys thinking?" Alicia yelled at her familiars.

They each pointed at Zoraida. She in turn purred.

"What am I going to do with you? We don't know enough about Valentino to trust him with our secret. Are you all insane? What would have happened if he'd seen you? How would I have explained a talking skeleton and a banished reaper living in my house as my official familiars? And you!" she said pointing at Zoraida.

"Oh relax. He didn't see anything. Besides who would believe him anyway. You worry too much," Zoraida replied walking away and going back to the windowsill.

"Fine, but if you guys are revealed and for any reason have to leave, I'm not going to stop you," she grunted.

"Sooo, how was your date?" Felix did a little dance that made all of his bones clatter.

Alicia couldn't help but laugh.

"You know I love you guys, right?" she said as she looked at all three of them.

"We know," Augustus said as Felix nodded his head and Zoraida actually purred.

Smiling she went to her favorite chair by the fireplace, sat down and told them everything. Well, almost everything. She kept out the electrical surge that went through each of them when they touched. She needed to do a little more research before she could determine what that meant if anything. For now, she was going to keep that little incident to herself.

She closed her eyes and thought about Valentino. Just as he sat down on his couch and thought about Alicia. Each smiling.

Chapter 15

Alicia had been working on a new spell for the last few days. No matter what she tried, nothing seemed to work. She furrowed her brow confused as to what was missing.

Meanwhile, Felix had been tapping his finger on the table and leaving behind tiny fragments. Augustus was pacing around in the lab bored.

"Will you two please stop fidgeting. If you don't want to be here, you can always head home," she announced annoyed.

"I was just wondering how long it was going to take before you perfected this new spell?" Felix asked.

"Yeah. I don't mind you working on your spell. I'm fine," Augustus tried to sound convincing.

"I love you guys, but sometimes you drive me crazy," she nodded her head giving up on trying to appease them.

"We love *you*!" Augustus yelled out.

Felix nodded in agreement.

The distraction was not helping matters. Then all of a sudden it hit her like a lighting bolt. Instantly, she knew the ingredient that she needed.

Alicia looked directly at Felix and as she slid her recipe book across the table she spoke.

"Felix, I know exactly what I'm missing," she stated.

"What?" he asked confused.

"You," Laura replied.

"What? What do you mean me? Are you going to kill me?" he asked flabbergasted.

"First of all, I can't kill you as you're already dead. Secondly, I would never do that to you. I care about you too much. Thirdly, well there's no thirdly, but if there were I'd tell you. Anyway, no! I noticed you tapping your finger on the table and realized you are leaving behind, tiny visible minuscule number of fragments," she said waiting for his response.

"Well, I'll be," he replied not finishing the sentence.

Sliding the finger several times across the table he gathered a small amount of bone powder and then looked up at Alicia.

"Will this suffice?" he asked.

"Yes, that's wonderful. Thank you," Alicia smiled.

The moment Alicia dropped the powder into the brew it huffed purple smoke indicating it had worked. She recited the new spell out loud.

Goddess of protection hear my plea,

Help me identify Sam's killer,

Give me a sign so that I know,

Goddess of protection hear my plea,

So mote it be

N ow, with the new potion she felt she was on the right track. She poured some of the ingredient into a new candle, one that she would keep in her office upstairs. The remainder of the brew she poured into a large glass jar and securely closed the lid.

Once she was satisfied everything was in order, she cleaned up the lab, turned off the light and went upstairs. Felix and Augustus followed.

Looking around to make sure no one was around she opened the alley door.

"See you guys at home. I'm going to lock up and head home in a few," she ushered them outside and locked the door.

Just as she was going to go back into her office, she heard a knock on the front glass door.

She wondered who'd be visiting this late at night. Couldn't they tell the shop was closed? As she approached the front door, she realized it was Laura.

Unlocking the door, she smiled and welcomed her inside.

"What a pleasant surprise. What brings you here on this breezy night?" she asked as she stepped back to let her inside.

"I was taking a walk along Main Street and noticed movement. Just wanted to make sure everything was alright here," she said as she looked around.

"Yes, I was just coming to pick something up I had forgotten," she replied.

No one knew she kept her lab in the basement and she wanted to make sure it remained that way. Luckily no one had ever asked where she made her candles. However, she was prepared to answer saying it was at home.

"Well, that's good to know," she replied looking around again as if searching for something.

"Did you leave something behind last time you were here?" Alicia asked.

"Why would you say that?" Lara replied.

"Oh no reason. It just seems as if you're looking around for something," Alicia answered.

"No. I just wanted to make sure there was no one else here," Laura said.

"I'm alone, why?" Alicia asked confused.

"There's something I have to tell you, but it's in the strictest of confidence. You must not tell anyone," Laura whispered.

Now Alicia was curious as to what she meant.

"Of course, you can count on me to not share any information," Alicia replied waiting in anticipation.

"Alright. So, the other day I was at the hair salon and I overhead Catalina saying some terrible things about Sam. She was in her office with the door ajar. I was on my way to the restroom when I heard her. She was saying something about being glad he was dead and finally she can now move on. I didn't want to appear as if I was listening so I kept going. When I returned, she was back in the salon. I'm not sure who she was talking to, but I wonder if possibly she could have done something to Sam or even Dolores for that matter," Laura appeared concerned.

"You know I did wonder if she had anything to do with Sam's murder. Maybe I should look more into her involvement with him and Dolores," Alicia stated more to herself.

"Well, if you need any help with your investigation, let me know. I'd be more than happy to see if I can find anything about her," Laura suggested.

"Thank you. Are you sure you're willing to do that? I don't want you to put yourself in any danger," Alicia responded.

"Of course, I'm willing to help. How could I not help one of my coven sisters in their time of need," Laura smiled.

"Great!" Alicia replied.

"I am curious though. Why do you think Sam was doing in your shop? Do you have any clues as to the reason or who would want him dead?" Laura inquired.

"Absolutely no idea. Nothing was missing so it doesn't look as if he was searching for anything. Although he could've been interrupted. The only think I can think of is maybe my spell book?" Alicia replied.

"Well, if that's the case, do you want me to hold on to it for safe keeping?" Laura seemed concerned.

"Oh, no. Thank you. My book is safely stored away," Alicia replied.

Laura wondered how secure her spell book really was and if having it with her was safe.

"Well, if you change your mind about me holding on to your spell book, let me know. You can trust me," Laura said placing her hand on her arm.

Now that it was said out loud Alicia thought more than ever, she needed to light that candle she had just created to see if the real killer would be revealed. Something told Alicia danger was close by and if she didn't do something soon, she may be the next victim.

Alicia walked Laura to the door and smiled as she held the door open.

"See you tomorrow morning," Laura said and with that left the shop.

Closing the door behind her and locking it she was glad to have a friend like Laura. Taking a deep breath, she double checked the back door to ensure it was locked. She then grabbed one of the new candles to take home with her and after turning off the lights locked the door.

Walking home she saw several of her friends and clients with their families. As she approached her house she looked over at Valentino's house. The lights were all off. She wondered where he was and what he was doing, but quickly put him out of her mind.

She needed to focus on the case and Haydee might be able to give her some clue as to what she needed to do next. Stopping at the house quickly to leave her stuff she told Felix, Augustus, and Zoraida she'd be back in a minute and headed next door.

Alicia's house stood in the middle between Valentino's house to one side and Haydee's house to the other. She walked up the stairs and knocked.

Opening the door, Haydee smiled.

"Alicia, come in," she said as she stood back with the door open.

"Thank you. I hope I'm not disturbing you?" she asked.

"No of course not. I was just watching tv. Would you like some tea?" she asked.

"Yes. That would be great, thank you," Alicia replied as Haydee closed the door.

"Make yourself at home. I'll be right back," she said and headed towards the kitchen.

A few minutes later Haydee returned with a tray. Setting it down she told Alicia to help herself. After she had served herself tea, she took a deep breath.

"What's troubling you?" Haydee asked concerned.

"I know I've said it before, but this case is driving me crazy. At first, I thought I knew who Sam's killer was. But as it turns out, I was wrong. Someone has now killed Dolores so that means she couldn't have killed Sam, right? And if so, then who killed them both? Is it the same person, is it two people?" I need help," she stated rather frustrated.

"Now, now. Let's see if I can be of any help.

Chapter 16

By the time that Alicia left Haydee's house she felt much better about where her investigation was heading. Although she needed to readdress her suspect list again and possibly interview them all over again, she knew she was getting closer this time to finding the real killer.

The next morning, she headed to the station to see if she could find anything out about the investigation. She doubted that Sheriff McDonald would help, but it was worth a try.

"Good morning, Alicia," the deputy behind the counter said.

"Good morning to you," Alicia replied smiling.

"What can I do for you?" the deputy asked Alicia.

"I was wondering if I could speak with Sheriff McDonald for a moment," Alicia asked.

"He's on a call right now. If you can wait, I'll see if he can speak with you when he's done?" the deputy replied.

"Sure. I'm just going to use the restroom. I'll be right back," Alicia said as she headed down the hallway.

As she approached Sheriff McDonald's office, she could hear voices. Slowing down her pace she inclined her head to listen. Sheriff McDonald had the caller on speaker.

"Yes, Sheriff that's correct. Dolores although was stabbed she died from poison in her system. We were very lucky to have identified the actual poison as some of it was in the palm of her hand."

It sounded to Alicia as the one speaking was the local coroner, Ralph Henderson.

"Now that's an interesting development," Deputy Donaldson said.

"Is there anything else you can tell me?" Sheriff McDonald asked.

"No. If anything else does come up I'll give you a call," Henderson replied.

Alicia scrambled to get to the bathroom before they realized she'd been eavesdropping.

So, Dolores was poison besides being stabbed. Now, that is a very interesting development, she thought to herself as she slowly closed the door behind her.

As she returned to the waiting area she acted as if she knew nothing about the conversation she'd just over heard and asked instead how everything was going.

Before the deputy could reply Sheriff McDonald walked out and as he saw her frowned.

"Why do you insist on bothering me?" McDonald growled.

"I'm sorry to bother you. I know you're a very busy man. I was just hoping you'd have some development on Sam's case. Being that it happened in my shop I wanted to make sure I'm safe there," Alicia replied.

"You know very well I cannot discuss the case with you. But if you must know, no there are no developments," he replied as he looked directly at her.

Alicia was about to call him out on his lie, but thought better of it. All she needed was for him to arrest her saying she was interfering with the case.

"I understand completely. Thanks again and sorry to bother you," she replied as she quickly left the station.

A few days later she was no closer to finding the killer. As she sat at the Cauldron Coffee House waiting for Laura and Meredith, she thought about the conversation she'd overhead and wondered who had access to poison and why did they kill Dolores.

Just then she jumped as she looked up to see Laura had placed her hand on her shoulder.

"Sorry, I didn't mean to startle you. I was just saying hi," she said as she sat down.

"It's fine. I was just thinking about something I overhead and didn't notice you come in," she replied

"Do prey tell. You know I love gossip," Laura laughed.

Just as Alicia was about to say, Meredith joined the table.

"Good morning, ladies," she said as she sat down.

"Alicia was about to tell me something that's she'd overheard that has her very concerned," she stated.

"So, tell us," Meredith encouraged her prima.

"Well, I overheard Sheriff McDonald speaking with Henderson about Dolores and the cause of death," she said and waited for them to respond.

"She was stabbed," Meredith stated as if it was an ordinary occurrence.

"Yes, I know. We found the body. What I learned was not only was she stabbed, but she was poisoned," Alicia said.

"What? Poisoned?" Meredith's mouth opened up as she mouthed the words.

Laura remained silent.

Looking at her Alicia asked what she was thinking.

"Doesn't that seem odd? Who would poison Dolores and why?" Laura asked.

"That's the one-million-dollar question. What I was thinking about when Laura came in was how to find out the kind of poison used. I don't know if it'll make a difference, but maybe knowing will help me identify the killer?" she looked at them for reassurance.

"You're right. Maybe we can do a spell to reveal the killer?" Meredith asked.

"Let's not do anything harsh. Why don't I check later today if there's a spell we can use. Meanwhile, you Alicia, don't do anything until we can reconvene again," Laura stated.

They all agreed they'd wait until she searched the Coven's database for a spell that would do just as they needed.

When they finished breakfast, Laura headed to her shop and Meredith stayed behind.

"I'm starting to get worried that there's a killer amongst us and we don't even know who it is. This is becoming more dangerous than I thought prima," Meredith was concerned.

"You're right, but knowing poison was used may be to our benefit if Laura can come up with a spell. So that you know, I didn't want to say anything because I'm not certain it'll work. However, I just made a few candles with a new spell. It's a protection candle against the killer. Why don't you stop by the shop and I'll give you one of the sample candles. I can't guarantee it'll work though," Alicia said.

"That's great. Yes! I'll come with you now and take one if that's alright?" Meredith asked.

"Claro prima, vamos. Let's go," Alicia replied as they headed out the door.

Walking towards Patchouli Mystical Tesoros, Alicia saw Valentino walking out of the bakery. He waved and she waved back. Feeling a bit awkward she looked down and continued to walk.

"What was that all about?" Meredith asked.

"Nothing really," Alicia replied obvious she didn't want to talk about it.

"Prima, I can see something is bothering you, spill it," Meredith insisted.

"Fine. It's just that I thought we had a great time at dinner, but he hasn't called me back. I don't know if I'm supposed to reach out or wait until he calls me again?" Alicia sounded frustrated.

Meredith laughed.

"If you try to figure out men, and especially him, you'll drive yourself crazy. The way he looks at you, I can guarantee he's interested. Give him a few days and if you haven't heard from him just call him. Or maybe even stop by the house with some *sample* candles," Meredith laughed.

"I know the way your brain works. I'm not making a love potion candle to trap him. Are you insane?" Alicia looked flabbergasted.

"Yeah, yeah. Fine. No love potion. But you can still call him. The worse that can happen is he says he's busy," she replied.

"We'll see. Anyway, let's go in I'm feeling a chill," Alicia said not realizing she was being watched.

As they entered the shop, Gertrude was just taking out the coffee.

"Good morning, ladies. How was your breakfast?" she asked.

"Delicious as always," Meredith smiled.

"I'll be right back," Alicia said as she nodded to Meredith's comment.

Sheriff McDonald entered the shop and greeted both Gertrude and Meredith. Looking around he asked where Alicia was as he needed to speak with her.

"She just got here, she went to the back and will return right away," Gertrude replied.

"Alright, I'll wait," he responded

When Alicia returned, she handed Meredith a package.

"Here, as promised," Alicia said.

"Gracia, prima," she hugged Alicia.

Just as Meredith was about to leave, Sheriff McDonald received a phone call. He briefly stepped outside to take the call.

In a muffled voiced he heard the caller say...

"The poison that killed Dolores can be found at Patchouli Mystical Tesoros Shop," the muffled voice said.

"Who is this?" he asked, but the caller had already hung up.

He immediately called out to his deputy.

"Yes, boss. What do you need?" Donaldson asked.

"I just received an anonymous tip stating the poison that killed Dolores could be found at Patchouli Mystical Tesoros. I finally have Alicia exactly where I want her," Sheriff McDonald said as he stood.

"Alicia? I can't see her as the killer," Donaldson answered.

"Well, if we find the poison at her shop then I have no choice but to arrest her. Let's go. I'm already here and will wait for your arrival, hurry," he demanded.

Sheriff McDonald waited outside. Once Deputy Donaldson arrived, they entered the shop.

"Welcome," she said with a smile.

"We're here on official business. We need to look around. Would that be alright with you?" Sheriff McDonald asked hoping he didn't have to return with a warrant.

"Sure, help yourself. By the way, if you still want to speak with Alicia, she went out back into the alley to empty out the garbage. She'll be right back," Gertrude replied giving them full rein of the shop.

They each nodded and took off in different directions.

Deputy Donaldson looked around the front of the shop while Sheriff McDonald proceeded to the back. Alicia had just stepped out otherwise she would have stopped him.

Sheriff McDonald knew sometimes perpetrators hid things in the tank of the toilet so he figured he'd start there. He was shocked when he opened the lid and sure enough, right there in a plastic zip lock was a small vial.

He put on his glove and extracted the bag. Shaking it to remove the excess water he carried it outside to the front of the shop.

"Where is Alicia?" he demanded.

"I already told you; she stepped out into the alley to through away the garbage. However, once she was done, she called me and told me she decided to walk over to the hair salon for a minute. Is there a problem?" Gertrude replied wondering why he was acting so authoritative.

Now Gertrude was worried as she noticed he was holding a clear zip lock with a small bottle inside. Donaldson walked up to Sheriff McDonald and looked at the bag and temporarily closed his eyes thinking there's no way Alicia would have done this. And, even if she was a killer, she wouldn't have left the evidence in a place where it could easily be found. But before he could say anything Gertrude asked about the bag.

"What is that you're holding?" Gertrude asked.

Ignoring her question, he demanded she call Alicia and tell her to get back to the shop immediately. Shocked at his tone she complied with his orders and called Alicia.

"Hey, what's up?" Alicia answered.

"Can you come back to the shop right away?" Gertrude asked rather shaken.

"What's wrong? What happened?" Alicia now alarmed by the tone of her voice.

Hay Dios Mio, que paso ahora. Now what? She thought to herself.

"Nothing happened. Sheriff McDonald is here and he needs to speak with you immediately," she said and then turned around and whispered.

"He found a clear bag with a small bottle in the back and is demanding on speaking with you, hurry," she said and hung up the phone.

To Sheriff McDonald she said.

"She'll be right here," she stood staring at the bag.

Within moments, Alicia entered the shop. Luckily there was no one there except Gertrude, Sheriff McDonald and Donaldson.

"What is going on?" Alicia demanded as she entered the shop.

"Alicia Whimblebright, do you know what this is?" Sheriff McDonald asked holding up the clear zip lock bag.

"Using my full name and all?" she chuckled then instantly realizing he was not joking.

"Sorry, no I don't know what that is," she replied still not realizing the gravity of the situation.

"I found this in your bathroom," he replied.

"And, what were you doing in my bathroom?" she inquired.

"We received a tip that we would find this here. I believe this is the poison that killed Dolores," he replied.

"Do you have a warrant to search the premises?" she asked.

"No, but Gertrude gave us permission to look around," he replied.

"Well, that seems to me a little fishy," she stated frowning.

At this point Alicia wasn't sure what else to say and since she couldn't let on that she knew the actual cause of death, she tried to act shocked.

"Wait did you say poison?" she asked as she brought her hands up to her forehead amusingly.

Gertrude chuckled.

"Ladies, this is no laughing matter. I believe this indeed is the poison that killed Dolores. And as such, am placing you, Alicia Whimblebright under arrest," he stated.

"Arrest? Me? I haven't killed anyone," Alicia now was worried.

"Yes. We'll sort this out down at the station. But for now, you must come with us," he replied.

Sheriff nodded to Donaldson and reluctantly he approached Alicia.

"Please come with me," Deputy Donaldson requested.

"Fine. But this is a big mistake," she huffed as she left the shop with Deputy Donaldson and Sheriff McDonald.

Immediately, Gertrude called Valentino and Meredith. Within minutes they were both at the shop.

"What happened?" Valentino asked shocked that Alicia had been arrested.

"Prima arrested? Is he insane?" Meredith said referring to Sheriff McDonald.

"All I know is that they walked in, asked if they could look around, and then the next thing I know Sheriff McDonald comes back here holding a plastic bag with a small bottle inside. He said it was the poison that killed Dolores," Gertrude said shaken.

"Well, clearly he doesn't know what he's doing," Valentino chimed in.

"I thought she was stabbed. When we found her there was a knife and it sure looked like that's what killed her. What do we do now?" Meredith asked.

"We find the killer and prove the evidence was planted by the real killer. Gertrude, come to my house as soon as you can close shop. Meredith, can you come with me now?" Valentino asked.

Before Meredith could reply Gertrude said she'd take care of her end.

"I'll close early and head your way as soon as I can," Gertrude replied.

"Let me stop by the shop and tell them I need to leave and for one of the girls to close shop today. I'll see you at your house shortly," Meredith replied as she left the shop.

Before leaving Valentino turned to Gertrude and assured her that everything would be fine. *It was time to do some magic*, he thought to himself as he quickly walked home.

Back at the station, Alicia was processed and placed in the holding cell.

"You know you're making a huge mistake, right?" she said to Sheriff McDonald as he closed the cell door.

"We shall see," he answered and then turned around and walked out towards his office.

Calling out to Donaldson he told him to personally take the bag to the lab for fingerprints and to find out what's inside the vial.

"If this indeed is the poison that killed Dolores and I found it in Alicia's bathroom, then we have our killer," he stated.

"Don't you think it's rather convenient that all of a sudden someone would call in with the evidence we've been looking for? How did this person know it was in the bathroom? Could this person have planted the evidence in the bathroom?" he said out loud.

Sheriff McDonald dismissed him without answering the questions.

When Donaldson returned, he informed McDonald he had dropped off the evidence and that they promised to have the results by tomorrow afternoon.

During the search, the killer had been standing at a distance watching. Satisfied they had found the vial and that Alicia had been arrested, they took a deep breath. As soon as Gertrude left the shop, they'd return to try and steal the spell book.

All of this would've have been avoided, if only Sam hadn't tried to steal the book for himself. And, Dolores, she too was inept and would've spilled the beans. She needed to be taken care of. Now, all that was left was to get the spell book.

Alicia sat in her holding cell trying to figure out who could've planted the poison. The shop was always so busy and many of the customers used the restroom, there was no way in determining who it could be.

Her thoughts were interrupted when she heard a commotion.

"I demand to see my cousin!" Meredith stated as she put her hands on her hips.

"Prima!" Meredith yelled.

"Fine. You have five minutes and then I want you out of my station," Sheriff McDonald demanded.

As he walked Meredith back to the holding cell she huffed and puffed until she saw Alicia.

"Prima, what is going on?" she demanded.

Looking over at Sheriff McDonald and rolling her eyes she answered.

"He apparently found evidence in my shop of the poison that killed Dolores. Without any real proof because it hasn't been tested, he arrested me. Oh, and he now thinks I'm the killer," Alicia said looking at Sheriff McDonald and arching her eyebrows.

"Five minutes," he grunted and walked out leaving them alone.

"Meredith, we don't have time. Tell Felix, Augustus, and Zoraida what happened. Felix knows of a candle I just made that will reveal the real killer. Tell him to show you where I placed it in the house. Light it, it will guide you. Please be careful. The killer is very cunning and will stop at nothing to get rid of anyone that gets in their way," Alicia said.

"No worries. I have Valentino and Gertrude on the case. Gertrude called us as soon as you were arrested. We're meeting at his place shortly. I'll keep you posted. And, as soon as it's dark I'll return to your house and talk to the guys," Meredith held her hand and sighed.

"Wow, Valentino is heading this? I'm surprised," Alicia replied.

"Si! Can you believe it? I told you he likes you," Meredith chuckled.

"Bueno, está bien. I guess at this point I have to believe if he's taken charge. Oh, you might want to invite Haydee. So, you know for now the suspect I had in mind was Catalina. I think she's hiding something and since I can't think of anyone else who'd want Sam or even Dolores dead you should all focus on her," Alicia replied.

"Times up!" Sheriff McDonald returned.

"Stay strong prima. Hablamos pronto," Meredith blew her a kiss as she left.

"Gracias, prima," Alicia replied as she closed her eyes repeating to herself over and over again to be strong.

As Meredith walked out, she waved at Sheriff McDonald.

"See you soon," Meredith smiled thinking to herself she'd prove him wrong if it was the last thing she'd do.

Chapter 17

Alicia was allowed her one phone call. She telephoned Sebastian who assured her he'd take care of everything. Within two hours Alicia was set free.

Laura arrived at the station shortly after Alicia had departed.

"I'm here to see Alicia," she stated.

"Alicia Whimblebright?" the deputy behind the counter asked.

"Yes," she answered.

"Oh, she was released a few minutes ago. You must have just missed her," the deputy replied.

Taking a deep breath, she thanked the deputy and left the station.

As Alicia reached her house, she noticed all the cars parked in Valentino's house. She was so grateful for her friends and family. Before heading over there, Alicia needed a few minutes to herself.

Walking inside, she closed the door and leaned against it trying to figure out who could've planted the poison in her shop. It was incredible to think that someone she probably knew well was a killer.

Just then there was a knock on the door. Assuming it was Meredith or Gertrude she opened the door wide and grinned.

Surprised to find Laura there she stretched out her hands and pulled her inside her house.

"Oh Laura, you won't believe what happened," she kept pulling her towards the living area.

"I actually stopped by because I heard you'd been arrested. Then when I stopped at the station, they told me you'd been released. So, tell me what happened," Laura asked.

"It was awful. I was at the hair salon when I received a call from Gertrude to come back to Patchouli's immediately. It seems Sheriff McDonald received an anonymous call telling him there was evidence in my shop linking me to Dolores' death. Can you believe it?" she sounded frustrated.

"Where exactly did he find the poison?" she asked.

"It was in the bathroom," Alicia answered.

"So, what are they going to do now?" she asked getting agitated. Slowly, she gulped.

"Laura, how did you know what Sheriff McDonald found was poison? No one knew that Dolores had been poisoned. Everyone thought she was stabbed," Alicia said as she stood.

"Sit down!" Laura demanded.

Alicia wiped tears from her eyes.

"How could you?" she asked shocked at finding out that Laura was the killer.

"Oh please. This is all your fault. If you had just shown me the spell book back when I asked you, I wouldn't have had to break into your shop and kill Sam when he caught me coming out of your lab," Laura was outraged.

Laura loomed over Alicia staring at her with such hatred Alicia recoiled.

Back at Valentino's house he was pacing the room as Meredith, Gertrude, and Haydee looked on.

"Where can she be? They told me over an hour ago that she'd been released. Why hasn't she come over. From what I can see there's no light inside her house. So, where is she?" he was frustrated and was beginning to worry.

"I'm sure she's upstairs relaxing. This has been a strain on her and she probably needs a little time to herself before she heads over here," Meredith stated while Zoraida purred.

"Alright. Let's begin without her. We can also catch her up when she gets here," Valentino said to the group.

They sat around the dining room table and discussed each murder and what they knew.

About a half hour later, they'd come to the same conclusion as Alicia. There was no way anyone in Wisterious Bay that they knew of wanted Sam and Dolores dead.

So, the question remained. Who was the killer and why kill them both?

Next door Laura had retrieved a gun and pointing at Alicia had been pacing back and forth making absolutely no sense.

Alicia was beginning to realize that Laura was not stable and if she didn't do something quickly, she'd be victim number three.

She figured if she engaged Laura in conversation, she might be able to convince her to turn herself in or at least let her go.

"Laura. Why are you doing this? I'm not understanding," Alicia said.

"Of course not. You who has it all," she replied flanking her arm around the room.

"You mean this house?" Alicia asked.

"Yes, for starters," Laura spewed out the words.

"I inherited this house from my father," Alicia answered confused.

"I know!" she screamed.

"Did you know my father?" Alicia whispered.

Maybe this had nothing to do with the spell book, instead it had to do with her father?

"Let's get some tea," Laura smiled ignoring her question.

"Tea?" Alicia didn't want any tea.

"Yes, you're going to have a nice cup of tea. Now get up and let's go to the kitchen!" She demanded as she pointed the gun at Alicia.

As she stood, she noticed the sun was setting. All she had to do was keep her talking long enough for Felix and Augustus to make their appearance.

She was certain Valentino and the gang assumed she was still in jail so there'd be no reason for them to come check on her. That meant it was up to her to keep her talking.

Laura walking behind Alicia had taken out a small vial she had in her back pocket. Frustrated to realize there was only a few drops she sighed.

This had better work, she thought to herself.

Laura intended to kill Alicia, then go to the lab and tear the place apart until she found the spell book. Once she had her hands on the book, she was leaving town before anyone could figure out, she was the killer.

Once they were in the kitchen, Laura instructed Alicia to boil water. After she placed the kettle on the stove Laura told Alicia to take a seat at the table.

Alicia decided it was time to try again.

"So, how did you know my father?" she asked.

If looks could kill, Alicia would have been dead right there and then.

"That vile man promised me this house and everything in it. Then he dies and leaves it all to you. This inheritance was meant for me! DO YOU HEAR ME!" she screamed so loudly Alicia covered her ears.

Then slowly when it looked like Laura had calmed down a bit she asked.

"I'm sorry Laura. I never knew my father and certainly I didn't know you and him were together. I'm sure we can work something out. Why don't you let me call Sebastian and I'll give you whatever you want," Alicia pleaded.

"No! It's too late for that," she said and the kettle informed them the water was ready.

Looking at Laura, Alicia waited.

"Get up. Pour some water in a teacup and come sit back down," Laura demanded of Alicia.

Alicia did as she was told.

"What tea would you like?" Alicia asked before sitting back down.

Laughing hysterically Laura answered.

"Oh dear, this tea is not for me. It's for you. So, you pick your favorite brand," Laura smiled.

"Oh," Alicia's mind was reeling.

She needed to figure out how to avoid drinking the tea. If she knocked the teacup on the floor, Laura might shoot her. If she doesn't shoot her, she'll make her get another cup.

What if she screamed? Would anyone hear her? Not worth it as Laura was still pointing the gun at her.

Closing her eyes, she said a little incantation and prayed it worked.

"I guess I'll have a chai," she said trembling.

"Good," Laura waved the gun again indicating she was to place the tea bag in the cup.

"Before you make me drink this tea, I need to know why you killed Sam and Dolores," Alicia asked.

"Fine. You'll be dead soon enough anyway," Laura replied.

Alicia placed her teacup on the table and sat down. Laura took out the vial from her pocket and poured the last remaining drops into the teacup. Looking up at Alicia she continued.

"It all started when I realized you'd inherited the house that was meant for me," Laura said.

Alicia already knew this, why was she repeating it, she thought to herself.

"Anyway, I knew that there was a lab underneath your shop. Your father used to dabble in magic down there. One night he took me there and said he wanted to share something special with me," Laura closed her eyes temporarily.

"So, my father used the lab for magic?" Alicia asked.

"Yes. When I was down there, he told he'd been working on a spell, one that would help me with my magic. You see, for the last few years my magic has been nonexistent. No matter what I tried, I couldn't perform anymore magic spells," she stated.

Now it was starting to become clear to Alicia.

"So, when he died and you realized he didn't leave you everything he'd promised you, you broke in to try and steal the spell," Alicia said out loud mostly to herself.

"Yes. That spell when I used it with your father made my magic come to life. All I ever wanted was to be a witch. Without my powers, I'm nothing," she suddenly stood and appeared angry.

"You're wasting my time. Now drink your tea!" Laura demanded.

"Wait. You haven't told me why you killed them," Alicia was trying her best to buy time.

"Fine. Things were not going well and for a long time I struggled. Then Sam came into town. He swept me off my feet. He told me Dolores was driving him crazy and he couldn't wait to get rid of her. At that point I believed him so I told him about the lab and the spell. He said he'd help me and we could leave this forsaken town together," Laura laughed a diabolical laugh.

"I gather that didn't go as planned," Alicia stated.

"Duh. Anyway, that night as I was coming back upstairs frustrated, I still couldn't find the spell I overheard him on the phone. He was telling Dolores what a fool I was and that soon he'd have the spell and they could leave town together. Can you believe it? The weasel was coning me!" Laura stood and started pacing again.

Patiently, Alicia waited for her to continue.

"I was so infuriated with him because he'd played me for a fool. While he was still on the phone, I went to your kitchen area and grabbed one of the knives. I waited until he had hung up the phone and then pretending to be upset got really close to him and stabbed him. The look on his face was priceless," Laura laughed again.

"I'm assuming at that point you wiped all the fingerprints from the knife and every inch of the shop," Alicia was nodding as she realized what Laura had done.

"Yes. Do you take me for a fool? I needed to make sure that even though my fingerprints could be found in the shop it would only seem as it was because I frequented your shop. Not because I killed Sam," she replied.

"So, why kill Dolores?" Alicia inquired.

"Dolores? I hated that woman," Laura now seemed angrier than before and Alicia found herself once again recoiling.

Chapter 18

"We need to start a search party," Valentino urged the group as he stood clutching his hands together.

Haydee looked directly at Zoraida and nodded. She made sure no one was watching and then she spoke to her directly.

"It's time," she whispered to the kitten.

Meowing Zoraida circled Valentino's leg.

Smiling Valentino bent over without even thinking and patted her on the neck.

"I need to talk to you," Zoraida said quietly.

Valentino stood up straight realizing that the cat had spoken. He started to laugh.

Of course, everyone except Haydee looked at him worried he was starting to lose it.

"Sorry guys. Just thought of what I'd do if I found out that someone had hurt Alicia," Valentino stated. It wasn't as if he could blurt out the fact that Zoraida had just spoken to him. It was obvious, this was not public knowledge.

"Well, now I'm afraid," Meredith responded.

"No. I'm not going to kill them. I'm just going to scare them into telling us what they've done with Alicia," Valentino replied.

"Oh, alright," Meredith breathed a sigh of relief.

"Now, you Gertrude, go back to the shop and look inside and around the immediate area. Meredith, you go around the station and see if Alicia left anything behind. You, Haydee, go home and stand by the window. Keep watch in case Alicia returns home. Me, I'll head out in a minute," Valentino gave out the instructions as everyone went their way.

"Don't forget to text us if you find anything. I'm creating a group chat so that you can respond there," Valentino yelled out as they walked out.

Turning towards Zoraida, he chuckled.

"So, I see you can talk. I knew there was something different about you," Valentino smiled.

"Yes. I've been keeping it a secret. It's not good to let people know that I can speak. Only Alicia, Meredith, Haydee, and of course Alicia's familiars know I can speak," Zoraida stated as she looked at Valentino.

"Wait. Familiars? What familiars?" he asked.

"You might as well know. Alicia's true familiars are Felix and Augustus," she informed Valentino as she licked her paw.

"Why hasn't Alicia or Gertrude told me about them?" Valentino asked confused.

"The reason is her familiars are only known to Meredith and me. No one else knows about them," Zoraida was starting to get bored.

"And why is that?" Valentino asked now becoming quite interested in this conversation.

"Do I have to spell everything out for you? Actually, I'm hungry any food for me? I can't work with an empty stomach," Zoraida meowed.

Laughing he told her to join him in the kitchen. Looking around he found a can of tuna, grabbed a plate and pouring it out placed it on the flower.

"We need to get going. So please can you tell me what's going on so I can go search for Alicia. I'm very worried she hasn't shown up yet. I feel something has happened to her and we may be running out of time," Valentino sounded worried.

"Fine," Zoraida said as she finished the last grub.

"Felix is a talking skeleton. Augustus is a reaper. All I know about him is that he was banished. Haven't found out the reason, but I guess that's not important right now. Anyway, they come to life at night. Soon, they'll be able to help also," Zoraida said.

"Well, that's rather interesting. I've never met a talking skeleton or a reaper for that matter. I'm looking forward to meeting them," Valentino said out loud.

"Alrighty then. I'm heading back to the house to see if I can wake them up. If I find something I'll let you know," Zoraida said as she walked out of the kitchen.

Back at Alicia's house she was curious about the spell Laura was intent on getting.

Still sitting in the kitchen and not having had any of the tea yet she asked.

"Laura, the spell my father promised you, what was it for?" she asked.

"It was to convince people to give me whatever I asked for. Mostly, I wanted it to make whomever I asked to give me money without any hesitation," she said.

"You were going to steal from the local townspeople in Wisterious Bay? Those same people that opened their arms to you and welcomed you into their community?" Alicia was now starting to get angry.

"Yes! You happy? Yes, I was going to take their money," Laura laughed again a rather maniacal sound coming out of her mouth.

"So, I gather you haven't found the spell. That being the case, why did you kill Dolores?" Alicia asked.

"Dolores," Laura spat out her name in disgust.

"Yes, why did you kill Dolores?" Alicia asked again.

"Because she had the audacity to try to blackmail me. Me!" Laura said angrily.

Alicia waited for her to continue.

"I knew I had to get rid of her. She apparently knew that Sam had made advances at me. She even laughed when I told her about us. They had planned it out all along. When I heard her laughing at me, I lost it. I left her house without another word," Laura said with disgust.

"Then what happened?" Alicia asked.

"I knew Sheriff McDonald had it out for you, and since Sam had been found in your shop with your knife in his back, I figured why not again? So, I went back to you place with the key I had and entered through the back door. This time I had gloves on. I went to the kitchen and retrieved another knife from your kitchen," Laura laughed.

"When I showed up at her house, she demanded to know what I was doing there. I tried to convince her to drop the threat. She wouldn't have any of it and just laughed at me telling me what a fool I was for thinking that Sam had any real interest in me," she said as she waved the gun around.

Alicia realized she was starting to run out of time.

"Before I continue, I want you to drink your tea!" Laura demanded.

"Can't we talk about this?" Alicia tried fruitlessly one more time.

"No! Now drink!" Laura stood and pointed the gun to her face.

Having no choice Alicia picked up the teacup and took a sip.

"If you don't drink the tea, I'm going to shoot you. Either way you're dead," Laura demanded.

Alicia closed her eyes and drank the remaining tea. Sitting back down she looked directly at Laura.

"So, I guess you can now tell me what happened with Dolores?" Alicia asked hoping she'd keep her talking.

"Oh yeah, Dolores. Well, I told her I would pay whatever she wanted. Then I offered to have a glass of wine with her to seal the deal. As she walked away, I poured the poison in her glass and waited. The problem was it was taking so long she realized I had spiked the glass and charged me. I had no choice but to defend myself. That's when I stabbed her," Laura replied and took a deep breath.

Alicia was starting to feel nauseous and the color had drained from her face.

Just then there was a clatter coming from the basement.

Abruptly standing Laura demanded to know who else was in the house.

Alicia was bent over with severe cramps.

"Now! Tell me who else is here in the house," Laura screamed.

"No one is here," Alicia whispered.

Not believing her she turned around and headed to the basement door. Turning the knob slowly while pointing the gun with her other hand Laura opened the door.

Chapter 19

Just as Laura opened the door Felix and Augustus reached the top floor.

Laura was so shocked she fell back and the gun went off hitting the refrigerator door.

Felix screamed and Augustus hid behind him.

"You cowards," Alicia said as she became ill.

"That's disgusting," Felix said without realizing the gravity of the situation.

Augustus was the first one to realize something was not right.

"What is going on here?" he sounded ominous as she approached Laura who was still on the floor.

"You're a…" Laura couldn't finish the sentence.

"Yes. I'm a reaper. My name is Augustus. Now, do you want to tell me and my friend here what is going on. And for heaven's sake why is Alicia getting sick all over the floor?" Augustus now demanded.

Regaining her wits Laura stood and pointed the gun at them. Augustus looked at Felix confused. Felix just shrugged.

As they stood there Zoraida entered the kitchen and knew in that instant what had happened to Alicia.

Going directly to her to check on her, she softly asked her if she was alright.

"Yes, I think so. Laura poisoned me, but I think she may have not used a lot as I'm still alive," Alicia said unsure of herself.

"I've got this. I'm going to get Valentino. Stay awake," Zoraida demanded and then scurried out of the kitchen before Laura could say anything.

Felix and Augustus had signaled to each other that they needed to take action.

While Laura was trying to figure out what to do with them, they approached her.

"Stay back or I'll shoot," Laura demanded.

"Are you insane woman? You can't shoot us. We're already dead. Besides even if you hit me, it'd only go through the bone. And, Augustus here is not solid so it'd go straight to the wall," Felix replied nodding his head.

"Well, then don't move!" Laura screamed as she turned around and faced Alicia who had decided to remained bent over in hopes that Laura would think she was more ill than she truly was.

Augustus reached Laura in record time and looking directly into her eyes whispered something that left her frozen. Her eyes bulged and she started screaming loudly.

While Felix and Augustus were dealing with Laura, Zoraida had gone looking for Valentino.

"There you are. Hurry, Alicia is at her house. Laura poisoned her," Zoraida said as she turned around and ran back toward Alicia's house.

Valentino immediately sent a text to the group and asked one of them to call the sheriff. Running as fast as he could he reached the house in record time.

He first looked through the windows to ascertain what was going on. When he approached the back glass door, he could see what appeared to be a reaper looming over Laura. A skeleton clapping, and Alicia was bent over trying to sneak a peek.

If the situation wasn't serious, he would've laughed.

He barged into the back door knocking the frame off the hinged and stopped abruptly when everyone looked at him.

"The cavalry is here, but you're too late. We have this under control," Felix spoke.

"You must be Felix," Valentino said as he walked over to Alicia.

"We finally meet. Yes, you must be Valentino," Felix clapped his hands.

Nodding he bent over and asked Alicia how she was feeling. At this point she realized Felix and Augustus could handle Laura so she sat up straight.

"A little wheezy. Laura here tried to poison me, but I think she didn't give me enough of a dosage, because all it did was get me sick," Alicia said as she pointed to the floor.

"No worries. You're safe now. The gang is on their way and they've called the Sheriff. You need to go to the hospital immediately," Valentino said as he tried to get her to stand.

"Wait. I can't leave her alone. Once everyone arrives Felix and Augustus must hide. No one can know about them," Alicia pleaded.

"Well, I guess the fact that you're speaking means you're probably right and the dosage just made you sick. But if they don't arrive within the next few moments, I'm taking you myself to the hospital," Valentino demanded.

"Agreed," Alicia said trying to smile.

"A talking skeleton and a reaper!" Laura kept repeating over and over again.

"Well, she's finally lost her crackers," Felix bent his headed up and down as if he was laughing.

Augustus stomped his scythe over and over again as he loomed over her never leaving her side.

Just then Meredith ran into the kitchen and realizing what was going on froze.

"I guess that's our cue to leave," Felix said as he nodded to Augustus.

"Yup," seems that way, Augustus agreed.

Looking at Valentino he asked if he could handle the situation until the police arrived.

"Yes. Go. Meredith and I will stay here and make sure Laura doesn't try to escape," Valentino replied.

"Let us know once everyone leaves. We'll be very quiet," Augustus said as they headed back down to the basement.

Closing the door behind them Valentino turned to Laura and realizing she was babbling, left her alone.

"Prima what happened?" Meredith asked as she ran to Alicia.

"Apparently, this is our killer and she tried to poison Alicia. But it seems she didn't give her enough of a dose to kill her thankfully," Valentino answered.

"Laura, how could you?" Meredith asked shocked at learning about Laura.

But Laura was in no condition to reply. She kept babbling over and over again about a talking skeleton and a reaper.

Meredith looked at Valentino and shrugged.

"Don't worry no one will believe her. If for any reason the Sheriff does, I have a spell to make him forget," Valentino replied.

Nodding she asked Alicia if she was certain she was alright.

"Si prima, I promise. I saw her only put two drops in the tea. Whatever she gave me was not strong enough," Alicia replied as the rest of the gang and Sheriff McDonald stormed into the kitchen.

Valentino pointed at Laura.

"Here's your real killer. She tried to kill Alicia today. She gave her poison, but it seems it was not enough to kill her. Although she needs to go to the hospital immediately," Valentino stated authoritatively.

Turning to Deputy Donaldson, Sheriff McDonald instructed him to take Alicia to the hospital at once.

"I'm going with you," Valentino demanded.

Deputy Donaldson looked at Sheriff McDonald for confirmation.

"Fine," he replied as he called in for more police.

Deputy Donaldson approached Alicia.

"Can you walk to the car?" Deputy Donaldson asked as he gently put his arm around her.

"Yes. But I'll carry her out," Valentino said ignoring Deputy Donaldson's question and Alicia's protest.

Deputy Donaldson could tell Valentino would not take no for an answer. So, he let him pick up Alicia and followed them out to his cruiser.

Once they were gone, Sheriff looked around the kitchen. That's when he noticed the gun. Retrieving a pen from his pocket he picked up the gun and handed it to one of the officers that had arrived.

He then approached Laura and told her he was arresting her for the murder of Sam and Dolores, and the attempted murder of Alicia.

It's as if Laura had lost her marbles completely. All she kept saying over and over again was that the skeleton and reaper spoke.

Sheriff McDonald looked at Meredith confused. She shrugged.

"She must have finally snapped. Talking Skeleton and reaper? She's insane," Meredith whispered.

"Laura, stand!" Sherriff McDonald demanded.

In that moment she focused her eyes on him.

"This is all Alicia's fault. I was promised this house and her father gave it all to her instead. Is she dead yet? You know I killed her right?" Laura laughed hysterically.

Taking her by the arm he cuffed her and led Laura out to his cruiser. Placing her inside he closed the door and turning to Meredith said he was sorry.

She just smiled. *Progress,* she thought to herself.

Once he was gone, she told everyone else to head to the hospital. She wanted to make sure all the doors were locked before heading out.

"I'll call my handyman and tell him to come right way to fix that back door," Haydee suggested.

"Perfect, thank you," Meredith replied.

"While you check the house, I'll sit out here on the porch to wait for his arrival," Haydee smiled.

"Thank you. Let me just go in and check on a few things. I'll be right back," Meredith walked inside the house and gently closed the door behind her.

Walking over to the basement door she opened it and called out.

"Coming down guys," Meredith said.

"What finally happened?" Felix was the first to ask as he walked up the stairs.

"Sheriff McDonald has arrested Laura. Valentino and Deputy Donaldson took Alicia to the hospital. Oh, and Haydee is waiting out on the porch for her handyman who's coming over to replace the back kitchen door. So, stay down here and don't make any noise. I'll let you know as soon as I hear anything," Meredith said to Felix.

Augustus had stayed at the foot of the stairs. She then closed the door behind her and searched the rest of the house.

Satisfied, she walked outside to the porch. She thanked Haydee and told her she'd let her know as soon as she got to the hospital how Alicia was doing.

Chapter 20

A week later, the front door to Patchouli Mystical Tesoros Shop swung open and Valentino stood there smiling.

"Ladies, how is everyone doing today?" he asked as he walked inside.

Gertrude knew that question was directed at Alicia.

"I'm doing great. I need to get something from the back room. See ya," Gertrude said as she walked away.

Smiling Alicia told him for the hundredth time she was fine.

"You never can be too sure," Valentino smiled.

"So, did you hear the latest? Haydee decided to take over Lotions & Things. Her latest spell is the hit of town. Who would have thought she could come up with something that made you look younger," Alicia laughed.

Laughing he said he'd see her later at the house. He needed to find a way to beat Felix at chess.

"Good luck. I gave up," Alicia responded laughing.

"Before I go, you have continued with your protection spell, right?" Valentino asked.

"Yes, don't worry. Even though Laura escaped I doubt she'd stick around here. I'm certain she's long gone," Alicia replied.

"As I already said earlier, you can never be too sure," he said as he blew her a kiss and walked out the door.

The festivities around town were in full swing. It seemed there were more tourists in town this year than ever before. That was good for business and Alicia was trying her best not to think about Laura.

The one good thing that came out of all of this was that for some reason Alicia's powers have become stronger than she even imagined. She doesn't know if it was the poison or the stress of realizing she might die or what, but whatever the reason she was grateful.

"Prima!" Meredith said as she entered the shop.

"Hola, prima. What's up?" Alicia asked.

"Just stopping by to see if you've made a decision about the magic school," Meredith asked.

"Are you sure you want to open up a school of magic?" Alicia asked.

Meredith just laughed.

"Fine. I'll think about it," Alicia smiled.

"Ready for lunch? I'm starving," Meredith said as she pulled her away from the counter.

"Hold on, I have to let Gertrude know we're leaving," Alicia smiled.

Walking to the back she looked in the kitchen and didn't see her. She then walked into her office, still no Gertrude. Thinking maybe she needed some fresh air she headed to the back door.

As she approached it, she noticed it was standing wide open and Gertrude was facing outside with her hands on her head.

"What's going on?" Alicia asked.

Just then Gertrude with her eyes bulging just pointed.

Alicia realized as she stood by her, why she had reacted the way she did. Not saying another word, she took out the phone from her pocket and dialed.

"What's your emergency," Bertha, the operator asked.

"You won't believe it, but there's a body in my back alley."

THE END

List of Other Published and Upcoming Works

COZY MYSTERY BOOK:
Rosa The Cuban Psychic Paranormal Mysteries

- Book 1: A Fashionable Fate
- Book 2: A Parisian Bait
- Raul's Demise (Prequel)
- Book 3: A Mysterious Date

A Wisterious Bay Cozy Paranormal Mystery Series

- A Wisterious Witch

A Tarot and Vintage Caravan Mystery Series

- Murder in The Campground

A Candeedo Brewdinkle Mystery Series

- Cipher, Mobsters & A Sphynx

Lolita Restoration Mystery Series

- If Walls Could Talk

Mrs. Greneerie Mystery Series

◆ Aunt Greneerie and The Missing Pocket Watch

The Shoemaker Mystery Series

◆ The Hidden Secret

CHILDREN'S BOOK:
Gizmo Adventures

◆ Gizmo Welcomes A New Baby

SHORT STORIES:
◆ Ghostly Gift, A Holiday Corner Cozy Mystery Series

NOTEBOOKS:

◆ My Tarot Journal
◆ My Notes - Las Cubanitas Journal
◆ My Notes - Cat Journal
◆ My Notes - Raul Journal
◆ My Notes - Candeedo Brewdinkle Journal
◆ My Notes - Abuela Nana from A Tarot and Vintage Caravan Journal
◆ My Notes - Dog Journal
◆ My Notes - Quirky Characters
◆ My Notes - Gizmo and Family Journal
◆ My Notes - Golf Journal
◆ My Notes - Rosa de Los Reyes Journal
◆ My Anxiety Journal
◆ My Aura Journal
◆ My Bird Watching Journal
◆ My Daily Journal
◆ My Notes Recipe Journal
◆ My Notes - Favorite Restaurants

Did you enjoy this book?

I f you enjoyed reading this or any of my other books, please consider leaving a review. Reviews are crucial to authors. It allows other readers an easy way to find their books. Here's the link where you can go and let others know what you thought about the book you just finished reading.

Amazon.com: Ileana Munoz Renfroe: Books, Biography, Blog, Audiobooks, Kindle[1]

Follow me on my various social media outlets including signing up for my newsletter. Also, don't forget to join our Birthday Club. During the month of your birthday, we'll send you a surprise. The Birthday Club sign-up is on my website in the same location as the newsletter sign-up.

Newsletter[2]
Instagram[3]
Twitter[4]
Facebook Author Page[5]

Renfroe's Reading Room[6]
Ghostly Gift – Holiday Corner[7]
Facebook - Cozy Mystery Village

---

2.   *https://www.imrenfroe.com/newsletter*

3.   *https://www.instagram.com/imrenfroe/*

4.   *https://twitter.com/IleanaRenfroe*

5.   *https://www.facebook.com/imrenfroe*

6. *https://www.facebook.com/groups/renfroesreadingroom*

7. *https://www.facebook.com/groups/holidaycorner*